WALKING
into the FIRE

Coláiste Íognáid, S.J.

Gaillimh

Gary Cross

WALKING
into the FIRE

Gary Cross

www.pearsoned.co.nz

Your comments on this book are welcome at
feedback@pearsoned.co.nz

Pearson
a division of Pearson New Zealand Ltd
67 Apollo Drive, Rosedale, North Shore 0632, New Zealand

Associated companies throughout the world

© Pearson 2009
First published 2009
Reprinted 2009

ISBN: 978-1-86970-649-4

Produced by Pearson

Commissioning Editor: Lucy Armour
Editor: Jan Chilwell
Illustrations: Adam Nickel
Page Layout and Design: Suzanne Wesley

Printed in China by Nordica

We use **paper from sustainable forestry**

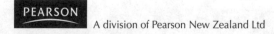

A division of Pearson New Zealand Ltd

AUTHOR NOTE

I've always been interested in the Second World War. When I was a kid, a lot of our dads had lived it. We took their battle honours as our own. Of course, back then, war was a game you fought in the back yard with plastic guns. Only soldiers got hurt.

As I got older, I got a wee bit wiser. I realised that war affects everyone. It peels away the layers to reveal the good and the bad – and in some cases, the evil. I guess that's what I've tried to get across in this book.

Many of the events depicted here actually took place in the Malayan campaign. I have changed the names and locations, but tried to keep the spirit.

War does terrible things to people. And makes people do terrible things.

Gary Cross

For my mother, who has
always valued friendship

Olivia Dempsey's world ceased to exist on the eighth of December, 1941.

The end came as a small black speck soaring high in a clear blue sky. It was such a trivial thing that Olivia didn't even notice it. None of them did. They were all too busy trying to stay awake while their teacher, Mr Thatcher, a white-haired rake of a man, ranted on about the wonderful flora and fauna growing rampant in the neighbouring jungle.

Olivia's eyelids started to droop.

The oppressive heat didn't help. She'd been in Malaya since her family had moved there from New Zealand when she was six. That was seven years ago and she still hadn't got used to the heat.

Olivia started when Mr Thatcher clapped his hands together. "Righto then," he said, in that posh English voice he had. "Let's get out there and see some of those little rascals firsthand, hey!"

The girl next to her let out a low groan. Olivia didn't need to look over at her best friend, Georgia Simmons, to know that right now she'd be rolling her eyes and pulling a face.

Twice a week during biology class, old Thatcher would drag his students out to the mess of jungle that bordered the school's playing fields to look at wildflowers that no one except him could care less about. It was always in the middle of the day, too, when temperatures were soaring. The heat didn't seem to bother Thatcher.

Now he was striding off across the field like a deranged stick insect, yelling to the girls to keep up and rabbiting on about what a glorious day it was.

Olivia looked up at the cloudless sky. And that's when she saw the plane – a funny, stunted thing, flying awkwardly in from the coast.

As she watched, it started to lose height. She could hear its engines now. An angry, growling sound.

"I think it's going to land on the field!"

That made everyone stop. All but Mr Thatcher, who was too far away to hear. He was still striding purposefully towards the jungle, intent on his beloved flowers.

Georgia waved her arms at the plane. "Get outta

PROLOGUE

here, you lunatic. This isn't an airfield!"

The plane came in low, barely clearing the steeple of the school hall. The engine had changed pitch. It was a deafening whine. And now Olivia could hear another sound – like a stick being beaten rapidly on a piece of wood. Takka-takka-takka.

Some of the girls covered their ears and screamed. Others just stood gawping. But Olivia's attention was riveted on the ground, thirty metres or so from the still oblivious Mr Thatcher. Puffs of dirt were sprouting from the earth and racing towards him in two neat rows.

"Mr Thatcher!" cried Olivia. "Watch out!"

The teacher turned, a puzzled look on his face, just as the rows passed across him. Then he melted into the ground.

The plane screamed over them. Olivia had a quick impression of bright red circles on the wings and an insect-like face staring at them from the cockpit and then it was gone.

For a moment, they all stood there in a bewildered bunch.

Georgia was the first to act. "Come on!" She grabbed Olivia and ran across to their fallen teacher. The spell broken, the other girls quickly followed. They formed a circle around the sprawled man.

Lana, the head girl, started crying. "Mr Thatcher! Mr Thatcher!"

"The plane! It's coming back!"

They looked up. Engines screaming, the plane zoomed in over the jungle canopy, coming straight at them.

"Run!" shrieked Georgia.

Everyone broke and ran. Olivia fled towards the school buildings. They were made of concrete and brick. She'd be safe there, but they were so far away!

The blood pounded in her ears and she could feel the sweat streaming down her face, stinging her eyes. She sensed rather than saw some of her classmates running alongside her.

And then that terrible rapping sound: takka-takka-takka.

Some instinct made her sprawl on the ground. "Oh please, oh please, oh please." She pressed her face into the warm wet grass.

Olivia felt hot air whoosh across her back. The plane's roar seemed to shake her body. Then the engines faded and became nothing more than a bad memory.

Someone was squealing. Olivia looked towards the sound. One of her classmates stood nearby, swaying, her eyes wide and staring. For a moment,

PROLOGUE

Olivia's mind went blank. Who was it? Who? Phyllis! That was her name. One of Lana's cronies.

It was Phyllis who was squealing. Her right arm fluttered bird-like in the air; her left arm hung limp at her side, blood dripping between her fingers.

"Goodness sakes!" Miss Fanshawe, the headmistress, lumbered into view, her hands pressed to the rolling flesh of her face. She swept the injured Phyllis up in her embrace. She looked around and signalled to one of the teachers who had come with her. "Get an ambulance, man. Quickly!"

The teacher scuttled back to the building.

Phyllis was moaning softly. Her skin had turned a sickly grey. Miss Fanshawe gently stroked her hair. "You'll be all right, love," she cooed. "Just you see."

She looked up. "Girls!" she boomed. "Come now. Gather round. We cannae stay out here lest those devils come back!"

Olivia's classmates, who moments before had been scattered across the four corners of the field, came to their headmistress, snivelling and sobbing, but alive.

Olivia scanned the faces. Her heart jumped. There was Georgia, coming in from the jungle's edge. Every few steps she looked skywards, her normally confident features now creased with fear.

"Come along. Come along!" Miss Fanshawe hustled them off the field. "To fire on defenceless schoolchildren," she muttered, more to herself than anyone else. "Oh, the shame of it."

"Miss Fanshawe," interrupted Georgia. "What happened? Who was that?"

"The Japanese, dear. The Japanese. They've invaded!"

Sirens sounded in the distance.

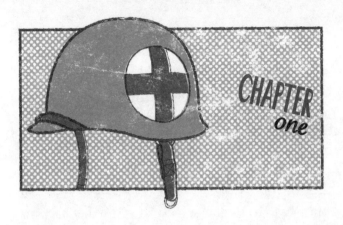

Olivia sat in the back of the car, chewing her nails and staring at the back of Ho Lap's neck. He was hunched over the steering wheel, carefully guiding her father's Bentley along the road. Army trucks filled with soldiers roared past on their way to the coast.

Ho Lap had arrived at the school barely ten minutes after the Japanese plane had disappeared into the clouds.

"Your father has instructed me to bring you home," he explained in his meticulous way. He was proud of his command of the English language.

He turned to Georgia. "You, too, Miss Georgia. Your father is at the house. He is discussing important matters with Mr Dempsey."

The two girls had piled into the oppressive heat of the car.

"Take care, my dears!" Miss Fanshawe boomed. She stood by the back door of the ambulance that had arrived to take Phyllis to the local hospital. Olivia waved, and caught a glimpse of Phyllis's ashen face as she was put into the back of the ambulance. Despite the heat, she suddenly felt terribly cold.

The car lurched forward as she settled back into her seat. Ho Lap was a lousy driver. "What happens now?" she asked Georgia.

Her friend just shrugged and stared out the window. It was obvious she didn't want to talk. And neither did Olivia when she thought about it.

And so they sat in sweaty silence in the back of the car, Olivia contemplating the back of Ho Lap's neck.

People's heads looked weird from the back. Ho Lap's was round and didn't have a hair on it. His ears stuck out and his face looked like a pile of ice cream that had melted in the sun – all soggy cheeks and double chins, so even when he smiled he looked sad.

Ho Lap was the Dempseys' houseboy. Funny that. A man in his forties being called a houseboy. House geriatric more like it.

Ho Lap and his wife had fled from Nanking in China when the Japanese invaded the city in 1937.

They had both been part of a Christian mission there, which was why their English was so good.

They had come to work for the Dempseys in 1938, after being referred to them by one of Mrs Dempsey's friends.

They never talked about what happened in Nanking. Olivia often pestered Ho Lap, begging him to tell her the details. It would make a great morning talk to her class. But Ho Lap would simply shake his head, get a haunted look in his eyes and say that some things were best left in the past.

Of course, that didn't deter Olivia and she'd kept at him until her father told her to stop. Mr Dempsey didn't want to lose Ho Lap. He and his wife did everything around the house. They cooked the meals and cleaned the rooms. They did the laundry and took care of the car.

Every morning, Olivia would get up and there at the foot of her bed would be her school uniform, freshly laundered and pressed. She'd go downstairs and Ho Lap would have her breakfast of fresh fruit, toast and hard-boiled eggs ready for her.

Olivia's mother never rose before ten o'clock. After a leisurely tea prepared by Ho Lap's wife, she would join her friends around the swimming pool down at the tennis club. Mr Dempsey was out on the rubber plantation at the crack of dawn, so neither of them had time to devote to such mundane things as housework or getting Olivia ready for school.

Olivia had never heard Ho Lap or his wife complain. They simply smiled and worked and spoke only when spoken to.

Mrs Dempsey didn't think much of them. In fact, she didn't think much of any Chinese or Malays. "Natural thieves, the lot of them," she'd say. "I really don't know where they'd be if we hadn't brought order to this country."

Olivia had heard her mother's sentiment echoed by many of the English expatriates whenever her parents had friends over.

Sometimes, when Ho Lap was cleaning the furniture, Olivia would deliberately leave a pound note on a table and hide behind a door just to see if he would pocket the money.

He never did.

The car slowed down, jerking Olivia's thoughts back to the present. They were pulling into a short dirt road made soft by the recent rains. On either side of them were the tall, thin rubber trees of her father's huge plantation. Off they stretched in ordered lines, as far as the eye could see. But Mr Dempsey was considered one of the smaller players in the market.

CHAPTER*one*

Some of the other planters had been here for years. It seemed as if they had divvied up half the country between them – they and the tin miners.

Rubber plantations, tin mines and jungle. For Olivia, that summed up Malaya.

Their house came into view a few seconds later. Like most European homes, it was a sprawling, single-storey affair. A veranda took up the entire front of the bungalow, its shade providing some shelter from the terrible heat. Wicker chairs and tables were set up in the shadows of the awning. Olivia could see her father and Mr Simmons sitting there now. They were talking to a man wearing a peaked cap and a beige-coloured army uniform. Olivia noticed a convertible car, painted beige like the officer's outfit, parked in front of the house. A soldier sat in the driver's seat.

Ho Lap stopped the car and everything turned to custard.

At the sight of her father, the emotions that Olivia had held in check since the attack came welling up. Tears streamed down her face. She flung open the door and rushed up onto the veranda.

"Dad!" she cried.

He swept her up in his strong arms and held her tight as she rattled through the events of the morning, then hid her face in her father's neck. She caught the smell of aftershave and Brylcreem. They reminded her of a quieter, safer time.

Eventually, Olivia's crying started to ease and her father gently broke their embrace and stood back from her, his hands on her shoulders. "It's okay. You're going to be okay."

Olivia wiped her nose with the back of her hand and nodded.

"Ho Lap's going to take you to the station," her father continued. "You're going to go and stay with your mother in Singapore until this little mess is over."

Olivia's mother had gone down to Singapore with Mrs Simmons five days ago to stay with Mrs Bathurst, an old friend from her mother's school days in England. It had been a bit of a ritual for the last few years. "To do some Christmas shopping," Olivia's mother would say. But Olivia knew that she just wanted to get out of Kota Baharu for a couple of weeks. She loved the bright lights of Singapore. It reminded her of her home in London, before she'd met Olivia's father, a young New Zealander with big dreams.

It took a moment for her father's meaning to sink in. When it did, Olivia broke away in shock.

"Singapore? But what about you?"

"I'm staying here. So is Mr Simmons." Her father flicked a glance at Georgia's father and then at the officer now standing next to him. Olivia regarded the man briefly. He was tall, with an angular face and cold blue eyes. He smiled at her. It wasn't very pleasant.

"But why?" Olivia turned back to her father.

"The Japanese have been sighted off the coast. Colonel Cummings here is taking his soldiers down to the beach to stop the Japanese from landing."

"But what's that got to do with you?"

"You know I'm a member of the local volunteer forces," Mr Dempsey replied. "It's my duty to go."

"Your father knows the area and he speaks Malay," Colonel Cummings butted in. He spoke in a clipped English accent, a bit like Olivia's mother. "Both he and Mr Simmons will be of great value to us."

"No!" said Olivia. "If you're not going, I won't either! I'll stay here with you!"

Mr Dempsey smiled and shook his head. "I'm sorry, honey. Anyway, it'll only be for a few days."

"Quite right!" barked Colonel Cummings. "Can't see those Japanese lasting too long when my lads get hold of them."

A roar filled the sky and they all looked up to see

a dozen planes, much bigger than the one that had strafed the school that morning. They were heading towards the coast. Olivia flinched, then recognised the insignia on their wings. A kangaroo inside a couple of circles – the Royal Australian Air Force. They'd been flying around here for the last couple of weeks, ever since the rumours of a Japanese invasion had started.

"See there," boomed Cummings happily. "Some of our air force lads off to give the enemy a bit of what for." He cupped his hands around his mouth and shouted at the planes. "Leave some for us!" Then, laughing at his own joke, he turned back to Olivia. "As your father said, this won't take long at all."

An idea formed in Olivia's mind. "Then they don't need you, Dad. They've got enough planes and soldiers to handle the Japanese. He just said so." She looked smugly at Cummings.

Cummings returned her smile and her heart sank. "As I said, miss. Your father speaks Malay. My chaps don't. He'll be useful in gathering intelligence from the locals."

"And I'll do that job a lot better knowing you're safely out of the way, Olivia."

A fresh wave of tears streamed down Olivia's

face. "I don't want Ho Lap to take me. Why can't *you* take me?"

"Colonel Cummings's men are waiting just down the road. We need to get to the beach before dark so we're ready when the Japanese land." He patted her on the back and she flinched away.

A hurt expression crossed Mr Dempsey's face. "Hey, hon. It won't be for long. You'll be back in a few days and everything will be back to normal."

An image of Phyllis's bleeding arm flooded Olivia's mind. Nothing will be normal ever again, she thought.

"Ho Lap's wife has packed a suitcase and a couple of lunches for you," continued Mr Dempsey. "Georgia's all packed as well." Olivia detected a slight tremor in his voice, and she almost reached up to touch his cheek, to say that she understood.

But then a little voice hissed at her from the dark recesses of her mind. Why should I, it said. He doesn't care how I feel. So why should I care about him?

And so she simply turned on her heel and stormed into the house for a shower.

When she came barging out of the shower, Georgia was getting ready to follow her in.

"I don't believe this!" hissed her friend angrily.

Olivia dried herself off with a towel and shrugged into a fresh blouse. She was already covered in sweat again. "Typical," she shouted to Georgia, over the noise of the water. "They never ask us what we want. They only do what they want to do."

"We're thirteen, for crying out loud! And they still treat us like kids!" Georgia emerged from the shower and dried herself off in a flurry of arms. She slipped into the white blouse and light blue skirt her father had packed for her and ran a brush through her blonde hair, studying herself in the mirror.

Olivia cast a sideways glance at her friend. She's so much prettier than me, she thought dismally. Where Georgia was tall and willowy, Olivia was short. Georgia's hair was blonde with hints of red that glowed in the sunlight. Olivia's was a muddy brown. In the sunlight it looked . . . muddy brown. Georgia had her mother's emerald eyes and delicate features. Olivia had inherited the features of her father and they didn't look quite right on a girl. Her nose was a little too long, her chin just a bit too strong.

Georgia was a born athlete. She was the best

hockey player in the school *and* the best tennis player. Olivia liked to think of herself as more of an academic. She couldn't hit a ball to save herself.

Another squadron of planes roared overhead and the windows shook in their frames. Suddenly, being more like Georgia didn't seem so important to Olivia any more.

The car was already packed when the two girls emerged from the bungalow.

Their fathers were standing in hushed conference with Colonel Cummings. Mr Dempsey seemed to be doing most of the talking. They hadn't noticed the girls' arrival.

"Hey!" called Georgia. "Do you want us to go or not? We're ready!"

Mr Dempsey and Mr Simmons broke away and hurried over to their daughters.

"Ho Lap has made each of you two cut lunches," Mr Dempsey explained. "You can buy whatever else you need on the train. Speaking of Ho Lap, where the heck is he?" He looked about and spotted the houseboy hugging his wife at the far end of the veranda.

"Ho Lap," he called. "Time to go!"

For once, Ho Lap didn't immediately respond to his employer's demands. He continued to hold his wife in a tight embrace, whispering something into her ear. She nodded slowly. Olivia was surprised to see her crying. She never cried.

Colonel Cummings cleared his throat and tapped his watch.

"Ho Lap!" Mr Dempsey shouted again. He was growing increasingly agitated, as if a few minutes could mean the difference between life and death.

"Give 'em another couple of minutes, mate," Mr Simmons said quietly.

Ho Lap produced a handkerchief from his trouser pocket and gently dabbed the tears from his wife's face. As he made to move away, she reached up and caught his arm. They looked at each other, but said nothing. Finally, his wife nodded and managed a weak smile.

Olivia regarded them with astonishment. She'd never seen them act this way.

Ho Lap brushed a strand of hair from his wife's forehead, then turned and came to the car. "My apologies," he said, nodding slightly to Mr Dempsey. His eyes glistened.

Mr Dempsey smiled awkwardly. "That's okay. Now, the way I figure it, you should be able to get to Kuala Krai by late afternoon. I suggest you stay at a hotel for the night and head back tomorrow morning."

Olivia looked at her father in surprise. Kuala Krai was far away to the south. The station at Tumpat was much closer. "Why aren't we going to Tumpat?"

"There've been reports that the Japanese may have crossed over the border from Thailand," her father explained. "Colonel Cummings says a couple of the Indian regiments have been sent north to deal with them but, even so, I think Tumpat could be a bit dangerous right now."

Olivia's throat went dry. The Thai border wasn't very far north. If the Japanese had crossed it, they could be here any minute. All the bitterness towards her father melted away. She lurched forward and hugged him tightly.

"You've got to come, too, Dad. The army doesn't need you!"

"Honey, we've been through all this." Her father prised open her arms. "I want you to go now," he said firmly.

"If you loved me, you'd come with me!" shouted Olivia.

Though her father recoiled at the outburst, his hand reached out to touch her arm. She jerked away.

"Leave me alone!" She clambered blindly into the back seat of the car, tears streaming down her face. Her father was saying something, but she couldn't hear him above her sobs. She huddled against the far door, her face buried in her arms.

"Olivia, honey . . ." Her father was at the window on her side now. She could hear the hurt in his voice, but she didn't care. Let him suffer, she thought spitefully. The way he's making *me* suffer.

She felt his hand on her head and she didn't flinch away this time. But she wouldn't look at him.

"I love you, honey. I always will." There was a brief pause. Olivia heard two doors slam as Ho Lap and Georgia climbed in. "I'll see you again soon."

"No you won't," snuffled Olivia.

There was a graunching sound as Ho Lap got the car into gear. And then she could feel the car taking her away. I'm not going to look up, she thought. The image of her father recoiling as she hissed at him sprang into her mind. And the pained tone in his voice as he expressed his love. Her determination wavered.

He just wants me to be safe.

She looked up. The car had reached the end of the driveway and Ho Lap was turning slowly on to the road. The house was out of view behind a stand of rubber trees. But he would still hear her if she shouted loud enough!

"Daddy!" she hollered. "I love you!"

She didn't know whether he heard or not.

CHAPTER *two*

One thing was certain. They were never going to make Kuala Krai by nightfall. Their progress south was painfully slow.

Time and again, Ho Lap was forced to the side of the narrow road as convoys of army trucks lumbered north, laden with soldiers. They were Indians mostly. And young. Olivia studied the fresh brown faces beneath the turbans and steel helmets. Many of them returned her gaze as the vehicles laboured past and Olivia could see the uncertainty in their eyes.

A gap appeared in the traffic and with a lurch the car was out on the road again.

A light rain began to fall and the warm breeze that wafted weakly through the passenger windows did nothing to dispel the almost unbearable heat in the car.

CHAPTER *two*

The rubber plantations had vanished now and they were travelling through thick jungle that pressed against the sides of the road like a green wall. Parrots shrieked and insects clicked and buzzed amid the foliage. Olivia looked at the tangle of vines and leaves. She remembered tales of people wandering barely five metres off the road and getting hopelessly lost in there.

"Do you think he heard me?" asked Olivia suddenly, thinking of her father.

"What?" Georgia had been lulled into a doze by the heat and the steady rocking of the car. She looked at her friend with bleary eyes.

"Dad. Do you think he heard me?"

"Course he did. The way you shouted, I wouldn't be surprised if the Japanese heard it in Thailand." Even as the words came out of her mouth, Georgia could have kicked herself.

Olivia nodded and managed a smile, but she couldn't stop thinking that her father might even now be fighting the Japanese. Georgia's dad, too. But they'd be okay, wouldn't they? They knew how to look after themselves. And they'd got half the Indian army there to help them. Then she thought of those young, uncertain faces staring at her from the trucks and her fragile confidence began to crack.

"It is getting dark," announced Ho Lap. "The blackout forbids us to use our headlights. I believe there is an airfield close by. It is where the Australians keep their bomber planes. Perhaps they will shelter us for the night."

"Well, we could do worse than a pack of Aussie pilots," said Georgia, in an attempt to lighten the atmosphere.

The sun disappeared below the jungle fringe and suddenly the world was plunged into shadow. Night came quickly around here. Not like at home, thought Olivia. You had time to get ready for darkness at home. But here – wham! One minute it's daylight, the next minute it's dark.

A white sign showed pale in the rain-soaked gloom. Great black letters announced: Royal Australian Air Force. 18th Squadron.

Ho Lap's sigh of relief was audible. Olivia felt the same. Ho Lap wasn't much use behind the wheel in daylight. She'd hate to be in the car with him at night.

He pulled into the road that led to the airfield. It was little more than a muddy track and the car laboured through the muck towards the airfield's main gate. A small hut stood off to the side of the road, supervising a wooden arm that was lowered across the gateway, preventing any vehicle from passing. Soon a figure swathed in a plastic slicker and holding a rifle emerged from the hut and trudged through the mud towards them.

The soldier bent down and peered in the driver's window. "And what do you think you're doing here?" the man asked in a thick Australian accent.

Ho Lap regarded him in silence.

"We were wondering if we could stay here the night," said Georgia.

The soldier leaned further in so he could see the girls in the back seat. "What's this, then? Out on a little holiday jaunt? Don't you know there's a war on?"

"Oh gosh! Really?"

Olivia cringed at her friend's response. She could see the soldier's eyes narrow in the gloom.

"Why do you think we're out here in the middle of nowhere? We're supposed to catch the train at Kuala Krai and go to Singapore. But, in case you haven't noticed, it's kind of got dark all of a sudden. And we're not allowed to put our lights on, which makes travelling a wee bit hard."

The soldier was silent for a moment. "You've got

a smart mouth on you, girlie," he said at last.

The tension hung thick in the air. "Maybe we should go," Olivia suggested.

"Like heck!" retorted Georgia. "I'm not spending the night scrunched up in the back of a car!"

"What's going on here?" Another soldier had emerged from the hut now and came striding towards them through the rain. The soldier jerked his head out as if he'd been stung.

"Civvies, Sarge," he said, his voice becoming a whine. "They want to stop here for the night."

"Well let them in, for crying out loud!" snapped the sergeant. He looked into the back seat. "I don't think they're spies. Do you?"

"No, Sarge," said the soldier weakly.

"Well, open the gate and send them through! I'm getting soaked mucking about out here!" He whirled around, sending a fine spray of rainwater into the car, and stormed back to the hut.

The soldier turned back to the occupants of the car. "Your lucky night," he sneered. "Drive along a bit and you'll come to an officers' hut. Report there."

"Thank you," said Ho Lap.

The barrier was lifted and he drove the car forward at a crawl. It was pitch black now, without even the stars or moon to give their light.

Somehow they reached the officers' hut. It was little more than a glorified wooden shack. A hand-painted sign saying OFFICERS' QUARTERS was nailed above a narrow wooden door at the front of the building. They could hear the rain drumming on the tin roof.

Ho Lap turned in his seat and looked back at the girls. "You go inside. I will get your suitcases."

Olivia waited for Ho Lap to come around and open the car door before making a dash for the hut. Still the rain soaked them both through and their legs were splashed with mud.

Mucky and bedraggled, they reached the door only to have another soldier appear from the darkness, brandishing a rifle.

"Hold up there!" Like the man at the gate, he was wearing a rain slicker but it didn't seem to be keeping him dry. "What are you doing here?"

Georgia fought the urge to say something smart. After all, it would only leave them standing out in the rain that much longer. So she explained again, as patiently as she could, that they were heading for Kuala Krai and needed a place to stay for the night.

The soldier looked them up and down then glanced at Ho Lap waddling towards them with the two suitcases. He leaned forward and opened the door. "Stay behind me," he said curtly.

They followed him into a sparsely furnished, smoke-filled room. Several iron beds were lined up on each side of the room and between each one was a rusty steel locker. Below curling photos of movie starlets posing in swimsuits, men lounged on some of the beds. They flicked idly through magazines or simply lay on their backs, smoking cigarettes and gazing up at the ceiling.

Another group of men clustered around a large wooden table in the middle of the room. They, too, were smoking cigarettes, adding to the haze hanging heavy in the air. Olivia resisted the urge to cough. The men looked exhausted under the harsh glare of the light, their eyes sunken, their faces sallow.

They've probably been flying all day, thought Olivia.

It was stifling in the room. All the men were in various states of undress. Some wore baggy shorts and singlets. Others sat bare-chested in their underwear. The sweat glistened on their skin.

The soldier who had let them in snapped to attention and saluted. "Captain Barrett, sir. Couple of civvies from Kota Baharu want to kip here for the night."

A tall, thin man in boxer shorts left the group

at the table and returned the salute. "Thank you, Collins," he said, his voice surprisingly soft. "You may go."

Collins saluted again and made his way to the door.

"Help yourself to a mug of tea on your way out," Captain Barrett called after him. "It's a miserable night out there."

"Thanks, sir," said Collins with a smile, heading towards the potbelly stove in the corner.

All eyes were now on the three newcomers. As the rain drummed on the roof, Olivia shifted uncomfortably under the scrutiny.

Captain Barrett smiled. "Forgive my appearance," he said. "We don't go in for too much formality around here."

"Too bleedin' hot for a start," piped one of the men at the table and a quick burst of laughter went around the room. It seemed to break the tension and everyone turned back to what they had been doing when the girls entered.

"There's a spare bunk down at the end," said Captain Barrett, pointing. "You'll have to top and tail, I'm afraid. As for you," he added, turning his attention to Ho Lap. "Grab yourself a blanket and find a spot on the floor."

Ho Lap surveyed the hard wooden floor, but said nothing. He walked down the length of the room and gently set the suitcases down next to the bed that had been allocated to the girls.

"Is there somewhere we can change and, um . . . ?" asked Olivia.

Captain Barrett seemed to notice their sodden condition for the first time. "Oh, of course. There's a bathroom in there." He indicated a door to one side of the room. "I'm sorry it's not the Ritz, but . . . " He shrugged, leaving the apology unfinished.

Olivia thanked him and the girls walked down the room to their suitcases. They could sense the men casting furtive glances in their direction. Despite the captain's friendly tone, Olivia knew they were not welcome here.

Armed with a change of clothes and their toilet bags, they opened the door to the bathroom and recoiled at the stench. Some of the men laughed behind them. Breathing through their mouths, the two girls dried off and changed and were back in the main room as soon as they could, taking deep breaths of the cigarette-smoke-laden air. It was better than what they had left.

The men at the table were talking animatedly about the day's successful bombing run against the Japanese. Olivia realised that these must be the pilots of the bombers she had seen flying overhead at Kota Baharu this morning.

Captain Barrett sat off to one side, staring into the middle distance and scratching his chin. To Olivia, he looked like a man weighed down by all the worries of the world.

Finally, he rose from the table. "We'll be going at them again as soon as the rain lifts. Time to hit the hay."

The group at the table broke up and headed for their beds.

Olivia and Georgia settled stiffly on their bunk. In their absence, Ho Lap had unpacked their lunches and Olivia picked up the neatly wrapped white wax paper, unfolded it and bit into the tinned beef sandwich. The taste reminded her of home and a terrible sense of loneliness swept over her. She stifled a sob.

"Hey." Georgia gave her leg a friendly squeeze. "You got me, pal. No matter what, you've always got me."

Olivia nodded, not trusting herself to speak. Georgia sidled closer and draped an arm over Olivia's shoulder.

"The Japanese have landed," Olivia said after a

few minutes of silence. "Do you think . . . ?"

"They'll be okay," replied Georgia. "From what these guys were saying, I don't think any Japanese even made it to the beach."

Olivia wanted so desperately to believe her friend.

They woke to the roar of engines.

Olivia heard a thud as Georgia tumbled out of bed, hit the floor and then rose, bleary-eyed, her long blonde hair hanging in a typical morning mess around her face.

She rubbed her eyes, scratched her stomach and did a huge stretch.

"Georgia!" said Olivia, horrified at the sight of her friend dressed only in her slip, for all the world to see. "Cover yourself up." She pulled a blanket up around her shoulders just in case she herself was showing more than she should.

"What's the point?" replied Georgia, nonchalant. "There's nobody here."

Olivia looked around. The room was empty.

Georgia padded over to one of the windows. "That's what all the noise is about. They're getting in their planes."

Olivia paused to put on a fresh blouse and

skirt before joining her friend at the window. The day was clear and bright. Steam rose from the surrounding jungle.

In the light of day, Olivia could see they were at one end of an airfield that was little more than a huge, muddy rectangle cut of the jungle. Several smaller huts were lined up alongside the one they were in.

Nearby stood three larger sheds – more like barns, really, with huge doors taking up virtually the entire front of each structure. Olivia could see the nose of a bomber poking from the interior of one of the sheds like some curious rodent. She could see trucks in another.

Steel drums, like the ones her father used to store petrol for the machinery at home, were stacked in huge piles at the jungle's edge. Scattered along the perimeter of the airfield and among the buildings were slit trenches, rimmed with sandbags. A huge cannon, its barrel pointed skywards, was nestled sentinel-like in its own castle of sandbags. Two men wearing steel helmets stood chatting in their makeshift refuge.

The noise of engines grew louder and louder and soon the runway was crowded with bomber planes. They were big machines, as big as the airliner that

WALKING into the FIRE

had brought Olivia and her family to Malaya seven years ago.

Perched high in each cockpit sat a pair of men. Even at this distance, Olivia recognised Captain Barrett in the plane closest to their hut. He was pulling his goggles down over his face. Olivia felt a chill as she remembered the Japanese pilot back at the school.

With that memory came a burning anger. Her teacher dead, her father who knows where, her home overrun. All caused by people she had never harmed in her life.

The roar of the engines reached a new crescendo as Captain Barrett's plane thundered along like an ungainly bird, sending great gouts of mud up from its wheels as it gathered speed. Finally, it left the ground and climbed skywards.

"Go get 'em!" shouted Georgia.

Olivia's heart pounded. Yeah! They picked the wrong guys to mess with this time!

Another plane took off, then another, until the whole squadron was flying towards Kota Baharu.

Ho Lap appeared at the doorway. "Ah, misses. I see you are awake. I have managed to arrange some

34

breakfast. I suggest that you come as quickly as possible and join me outside."

After Georgia had dressed, the two girls followed Ho Lap to another hut where the aroma of cooked eggs greeted them at the door. It was crowded with men eating breakfast at long tables.

Ho Lap directed them to a table where a portly man dressed in a grease-stained singlet was dishing out food from two large pots. He ladled scrambled eggs and baked beans on to the girls' plates then dumped a thick slice of bread atop each steaming mound of food.

Ho Lap found them three empty seats at the end of one of the long tables. The men closest to them regarded the newcomers with brief curiosity, then went back to shovelling food into their mouths.

What a mangy-looking lot, thought Olivia. They were covered in muck and grease. A couple of them wore filthy bib-style overalls, but most were bare-chested. Sweat carved little waterways through the grime on their bodies.

Exhaustion hung heavy on these men, as it had on the pilots last night. Unlike the pilots, however, they showed no signs of bravado as they talked in low, tired tones.

"These gentlemen are the ground crew," explained Ho Lap. "They refuel the bombers and put in new bombs after every flight."

The man sitting next to them laughed grimly. "We do all the work. The flyboys get all the glory."

"Don't know why we're bothering anyway," said another. "The Japanese are probably already off the beaches."

Olivia felt her body go cold.

"Too right they'll be off the beaches! Probably heading this way right now!"

A thin, sparrow-faced man joined in the conversation. "I don't know why the Poms didn't put more people in the front line. Useless, if you ask me."

"It's all they've got, mate," the second man retorted. "Least until they can get our blokes up from Singapore."

"Be too late by then though, won't it?" It was the first man again, relishing his role as the harbinger of doom. He was almost shouting now, so that everyone in the room could hear. "The Japanese will be all over the place. I tell you, we shoulda pulled out last night. Beggared off to one of the airfields further south, instead of sticking it out here. We're nearly on the front line, for crying out loud!"

There were murmurs of agreement.

The mood of the room had turned ugly and Olivia didn't feel hungry any more. She put the fork down on her plate. "I think we should go soon," she said softly to her companions.

Georgia nodded, chewing the last mouthful from her plate.

As they got up to leave, Olivia found herself face to face with the surly soldier they had encountered at the gate last night. Up close, she could see the acne covering his face. His breath was sour.

"Leaving so soon?" he sneered.

Olivia was about to tell him to shove off when a high-pitched scream filled the air. There was a tremendous explosion and all the windows in the room shattered inwards. Shards of glass flew through the air. Men screamed.

A man burst through the door, fear on his face. "The Japanese!" he screamed. "The . . ." His words were drowned out by another explosion, much closer this time. The whole room seemed to shake.

"Get to the trenches!" someone shouted.

The men stampeded towards the door and someone pushed Olivia in the back. She tumbled to the floor and felt a sharp pain as a running crewman knocked her in his haste to get away. Another foot glanced off her skull and her head swam.

Someone grabbed her arm and hauled her to her feet. It was Ho Lap. His mouth was opening and closing, but her ears were ringing so much she couldn't hear a word he was saying. She shook her head and he nodded. Then Georgia grabbed her other arm and they turned to follow the fleeing men.

The air was filled with the piercing whine of falling bombs. Explosions rent the ground, throwing up great waves of mud. One of the huts was already flattened. With an ear-numbing roar, another exploded into countless pieces. Timber and glass cascaded around them, but by some miracle they weren't hit.

"The slit trenches! Over there!" yelled Georgia, pointing at a group of running men.

From the corner of her eye, Olivia saw the stack of petrol barrels turn into a gigantic fireball and felt the heat of the blast on her cheek. All three of them stumbled under the force of the explosion and then the sky was raining barrels of fire.

They ran, ducking and weaving as barrels crashed to the ground around them, spraying liquid flame.

The ground opened up beneath Olivia and she tumbled face first into foul-smelling water. It filled her mouth and clogged her throat and she came up coughing and spluttering. She was at the bottom of a trench, up to her knees in muddy water that rippled and surged as the bombs continued to fall.

She looked up. High above, Japanese bombers filled the sky like swarms of malignant birds. Formation after formation droned past, sending their deadly cargo earthwards. Olivia could see little puffs of black smoke appear around the planes as the lone anti-aircraft gun fired back. It failed to hit a single plane.

Why couldn't the idiots shoot straight?

The explosions went on and on. Around them in the crowded trench, some men were sobbing. Others shook their fists and shouted obscenities at the aircraft.

As if they can hear, thought Olivia.

The air raid finished as suddenly as it had begun. For several moments, everyone was still. Someone in the trench was still crying, but out on the field there were other sounds. Much louder. The sounds of men in pain.

One by one, the Australian ground crew clambered out of the trench. Olivia felt a hand on her shoulder and realised that she had been pressing her face against the side of the trench. She wiped the muck from her eyes and mouth.

"I think it is safe to get out now, miss," said Ho Lap. "The Japanese planes have gone."

Olivia's legs felt weak as she hauled herself out of the trench. Her whole body was shaking.

"Do you think they'll be back?" She felt a flush of shame at the tremor in her voice.

The man closest to them shot her a look. "Too right they'll be back. And sharpish, too, I shouldn't wonder."

"Well I'm beggared if I'm hanging around waiting for them." It was the sparrow-faced man. He was bleeding from a gash in his arm. "Let's get the heck out of here!"

A chorus of voices roared their approval, but a few looked doubtful. "I dunno," said one. "What about when Barrett gets back?"

Sparrow Face snorted. "What's he gonna come back to?" He gestured at the smoking ruin that had been an airfield only minutes before.

Wounded men wandered aimlessly through the smoke and ruins. Others lay on the ground, some filling the air with their groans, some remaining ominously quiet.

"He's right," said someone. "For all we know, the Japanese army could be just through those trees!"

The men cast nervous glances at the jungle.

But it wasn't the jungle they had to worry about. With a snarl, a Japanese fighter plane, sleek and deadly in the sunlight, burst over a line of trees and dived towards the airfield.

The plane roared past, executed a steep bank and dived back to wreak more havoc. One of the trucks erupted into flame and the man who had been sitting in the driver's seat leapt out, his clothes smoking. He rolled around in the mud, yelling and cursing.

A ghastly silence fell as the plane disappeared over the tree line and, for several seconds, no one dared get up.

Sparrow Face was the first to rise. "That's it!" he declared in a shaky voice. "I'm outta here!"

His companions needed no further prompting. They broke and ran. The panic swept up everyone on the airfield like a wave. Within seconds, anyone who could run was heading towards the remaining trucks. Some had the presence of mind to carry those wounded who were unable to walk.

Ho Lap watched the panic for a moment then turned to the girls. How calm he looks, thought Olivia. Amid all this turmoil, he looks just the same as he always does.

"I suggest we make our way to the car as quickly as possible." He began shepherding them towards the officers' hut. The Bentley still stood nearby, exactly where Ho Lap had parked it the night before. The bombs hadn't touched it.

Ho Lap hurried over and opened the back door for the girls. A truck roared past, crowded with men. Others followed.

Men raced past on foot, some pulling on shirts as they ran.

"Our suitcases!" cried Olivia.

"Get into the car," said Ho Lap, raising his voice to be heard over the din of traffic. "I will get them."

He disappeared into the hut. More men shot past, yelling at the trucks to slow down. One screeched to a halt and hands reached down to haul the running men aboard.

A mud-covered man dressed in khaki shorts and a dirty white singlet skidded to a halt by the car. He peered in and rubbed his chin.

"Clear off!" yelled Georgia.

The man started, paused for a moment, then took off like a startled rabbit. But there'd be more, thought Olivia. All the trucks have gone and they'll want the car. Oh, hurry up, Ho Lap. Hurry up!

She reached over and squeezed Georgia's hand.

"Don't worry," said her friend, as feisty as ever. "I'll clout the first berk who sticks his head in."

When Ho Lap reappeared, Olivia let out a loud sigh of relief. He piled the cases on the front seat, slammed the door and turned on the ignition.

He froze as a face appeared at the open window.

"Trip's over, mate," hissed the pimply soldier with the sour breath. He flicked his eyes at the girls. "Get out, the lot of you."

Sweat poured down his face. His eyes were wide and white and his mouth curled back in an ugly sneer. A loud huffing sound came from his flared nostrils, like a bull getting ready to charge.

Olivia reached for the door handle, but Ho Lap's calm, level voice stopped her. "Stay where you are, miss. We are not surrendering our vehicle to this man."

The soldier's eyes grew even wider with disbelief. "What did you say?" His voice rose to a squeak.

"I made a promise to these girls' fathers that I would deliver them safely to the railway station at Kuala Krai," said Ho Lap, looking straight ahead. "I will not permit a cringing coward like yourself to prevent me from performing that task." He graunched the car into gear.

"Get out of that car, you git! Or I'll finish you, so help me!"

Olivia saw his knuckles whiten on the rifle in his hands.

Ho Lap remained sitting in his seat, his face calm.

Seizing her chance, Olivia threw the door open, knocking the soldier off balance. She leapt out of the car and flung open Ho Lap's door.

"Get out!" she shouted. "Now!"

He looked at her, but still he wouldn't move. Olivia could hear the snap of the rifle bolt being pushed home behind her. "It's not worth it," she said, looking Ho Lap directly in the eye. "He'll kill you and we'll be left all alone and you will have broken your word to my father. Please, Ho Lap, get out. Let him have the car."

Olivia felt tears trickle warm and wet down her cheeks. "Please," she implored, her voice barely a whisper. "Please."

At last Ho Lap nodded slightly, turned off the ignition and climbed out. He reached back and dragged out the suitcases. The pimply soldier pushed him hard to the ground and Ho Lap grunted with pain as the suitcases tumbled over him.

"You sod!" Georgia was out of the car now. She

came around Olivia, ready to throw herself at the soldier. But there was something in his eyes that melted even her courage, something slightly off centre. "Don't push your luck," he said, his voice dripping with menace.

Shooting the girls a final malevolent look, the soldier climbed into the driver's seat and switched on the ignition.

"Maybe I'll see you in Singapore!" He laughed and floored the accelerator. With a roar, the Bentley was off, spraying the girls with mud.

"You'd better hope you don't see us in Singapore, you gutless wonder!" raged Georgia after the disappearing vehicle.

With a final screech of tyres, the car turned on to the road and hurtled away, the roar of its engine growing steadily quieter until there was only the sound of the jungle.

They were alone on the ruined airfield.

Ho Lap winced as he forced himself to his feet.

"I can't believe that guy!" raged Georgia. "I thought the army was supposed to protect us. Not pinch our car and head for the hills!"

"He is a frightened man," said Ho Lap, still slightly breathless. "It takes more than a uniform to make him brave."

Olivia looked up at the cloudless sky, expecting to see more Japanese fighters come screaming down at any moment. But the blue expanse remained empty.

The planes had come from the north. Maybe what the Australians had said was true? What if the Japanese army was even now marching south through the jungle towards them?

That would mean Kota Baharu had been taken. Father . . .

"We've got to go back," she said.

"What?" snapped Georgia.

"We've got to go back," repeated Olivia, more forcefully this time. "We've got to go back and find our fathers!"

"Oh . . . Oh yes." The reality started to dawn on Georgia. "You're right."

Ho Lap shook his head. "No," he said flatly.

Olivia whirled on him. "How dare you say no to me! I said we've got to go back! You've got to take us back to our fathers!"

"My wife and I, we had a daughter slightly younger than you are now," said Ho Lap evenly, as if he had not heard her tirade. He paused, his eyes seeing not them but something that had happened years before. "She died when the Japanese captured

Nanking. We were separated briefly. In all the confusion, you know."

Olivia stood there, her mouth agape with surprise.

"They shot her. The soldiers shot her."

Georgia made a squawking sound.

"Before we escaped from the city, we saw what the Japanese soldiers did to the women and children." Ho Lap's voice was flat and emotionless, which made his tale so much worse. He fixed Olivia with a steady gaze. "Believe me. You do not want to return to Kota Baharu. Not if the Japanese are there."

Olivia's anger melted beneath that steely stare. She wanted to protest, more out of hurt pride than anything, but he cut her off.

"They will do the same to you, both of you, if they catch you."

Olivia's throat went dry and any last shred of resistance crumbled at the horror implied in Ho Lap's words. "But your wife . . ." she said thickly.

"I am confident that your fathers have taken her to a place of safety. They are both resourceful men. As for you, I will take you to Kuala Krai where it is safe. As I promised your fathers."

"But how?"

"We walk," he said simply. He picked up the girls'

suitcases, one in each hand, and set off towards the gate, his round, hairless head held high, his ears sticking out like badges of pride.

Olivia and Georgia watched him for a moment. He looked so funny, waddling along. But there was something noble about him, too. Something that Olivia had never before seen in the man.

"I didn't know he had a daughter," whispered Georgia.

Thunder rumbled to the north. Or was it the sound of guns?

CHAPTER three

Olivia woke up covered in sweat and bugs. Something long and multi-legged was crawling across the back of her neck.

She screamed and jumped to her feet and whatever it was dropped from her neck and down her back. "Squash it!" she hollered, flailing and squirming. "Squash it!"

Georgia looked up sleepily from her bed of palms on the ground and watched for a moment as Olivia capered about, her arms flapping in a useless effort to get at the creature. Finally, she hauled herself up – far too casually for Olivia's liking – and whacked Olivia hard on the back with the flat of her hand.

Something warm and sticky splattered over her skin.

"Got it!" hooted Georgia triumphantly.

Olivia pulled off her blouse. It was drenched with

mud, sweat and now the green goo of some jungle insect. "Wipe it off, will you?"

Georgia pulled a face. "It was big, whatever it was!" She grabbed Olivia's blouse and wiped her back with it. "There. Not too bad," she said with a smile and handed the filthy garment back. Olivia threw it into the thick undergrowth. She wouldn't be wearing that again.

She opened her suitcase and rummaged around. Only two fresh outfits left, she noted with dismay.

"Don't know why we had to sleep in the jungle in the first place," she grumbled, struggling into a new blouse. It stuck uncomfortably to her grimy skin.

"Didn't hear you complaining when Ho Lap suggested it," said Georgia, using her suitcase as a seat.

"Yeah, well . . ."

It *had* seemed like a good idea at the time. They'd been walking for three hours since leaving the airfield. The first half-hour or so hadn't been too bad, but after that it was hard slog. The sun had blazed down, sapping their energy so that each step became an effort. There was no wind to relieve the heat.

Often they had to scuttle for cover in the steaming jungle as Japanese bombers roared southwards in great swarms.

CHAPTER *three*

Olivia wondered what had happened to Captain Barrett. Had he made it to another airfield?

Sometimes they heard the thump of explosions in the distance, and Olivia pitied whoever was beneath that storm of bombs. And sometimes they could see talons of black smoke reaching up into the still, blue sky.

Soon they came across evidence of the Japanese bombing. Explosions had gouged great wounds in the road and the charred wreckage of trucks, cars and little armoured vehicles was scattered about. There was no sign of bodies. For that, Olivia was grateful.

Sweat was now her constant companion. She could feel it running like a miniature waterfall down her front and back. She had loosened her blouse, but that offered no relief at all. Her face burned. Her legs ached.

The mud from the trench had long since dried on her legs, forming a hard, itchy second skin. Her sodden shoes chafed at the backs of her heels.

"How much further?" Georgia would ask. At first it was every twenty minutes. Then every ten, until it seemed as if she was asking with every step they took.

Ho Lap's answer was always the same. "Not far now, misses."

The journey hadn't seemed to affect him at all, Olivia noticed. He was still walking along, suitcases swinging in both hands, his step strong and confident.

She looked over at Georgia. At least she looks as bad as I feel, she thought with childish satisfaction.

Finally, Olivia could take it no longer. "I need to rest!" she gasped.

"Too right!" echoed Georgia. "We're done for, Ho Lap. Give us a break, will you?"

Ho Lap stopped and nodded. He walked over to the jungle fringe, found a spot that wasn't as dense as the rest, and set the suitcases down. "Rest here," he said. "Make sure you are out of sight of the road. I will search ahead to see if there is a village nearby."

The girls were asleep as soon as their heads hit the soft jungle floor.

Olivia wasn't sure how long they had slept. Probably not long. The sun didn't seem to have moved much and she felt every bit as tired and dirty as before.

"I'm parched," said Georgia, sticking her tongue out. "I hope Ho Lap's managed to find us some water."

As if on cue, Ho Lap emerged from the foliage.

A faint sheen of sweat on his forehead was the only indication that maybe he did feel the heat after all.

"There is a village close by," he said. "Just off the main highway. There are English soldiers there, too. With luck we will be able to travel with them to Kuala Krai."

"As long as they've got some fresh water, that's all I care about." Georgia heaved herself to her feet.

"I'm sure that can be arranged," replied Ho Lap.

The two girls followed him back to the road. Two hundred metres on, they came to a muddy track, just wide enough for one vehicle. Ho Lap led the way down this side road and they soon came to a small cluster of wooden shacks.

Village is too good a word for it, thought Olivia despondently. She hoped the soldiers carried enough water with them, because it didn't look as if this place had anything to offer that was fit to drink.

A couple of army trucks were parked in what passed for a street and an officer stood talking to a couple of soldiers. There was no sign of any villagers. The trio of men looked over as Olivia and her companions approached. Olivia saw with surprise that one of the men pointed his rifle in their direction. He wasn't exactly aiming it, but it was unnerving just the same.

The officer stepped forward to meet them. He was a stocky man, with a ruddy face and a thin black moustache. His eyes were like small raisins. They studied the newcomers coldly.

"Where on earth did you lot appear from?" he asked in an upper-crust English accent.

"We are from Kota Baharu," explained Ho Lap. "I was taking these girls to the station at Kuala Krai when our vehicle was . . . taken away from us."

The officer snorted. "Got to be careful with all these natives about."

"It wasn't natives who took it," said Georgia. "It was a bunch of Aussies. From the airfield north of here."

The officer's eyes widened in surprise then narrowed again. "You mean the Japanese have taken the airfield?"

"Dunno about that," replied Georgia. "But our side has certainly left it."

"Well, that's put a spanner in the works," mused the officer quietly. "No point in carrying on north now. We may as well turn back."

"I was wondering if we could get a ride with you to Kuala Krai," asked Ho Lap.

"Sorry, no room," said the officer in a voice that offered no room for argument either. "You civvies will have to look after yourselves, I'm afraid." He shook his head. "What a mess."

"But these girls . . ." protested Ho Lap.

The officer shot him a withering look. "I said there was no room. Keep going south. You're bound to come across a car or truck or something that has some space."

"Perhaps you could share some of your water with the young ladies at least?"

The officer studied the two girls for a moment, then signalled to the soldiers nearby. "Hawkins! Gamble! Give the girls here your canteens."

The two soldiers obeyed. They didn't look too happy about it.

"Captain!" A soldier came running up the street and staggered to a halt in front of the officer, saluting. "Captain Hall, sir. We've found some more spies, sir. Caught 'em red-handed signalling to the Japanese planes."

"Show me," said Captain Hall grimly.

They trudged back down the street. Curious, Olivia and Georgia fell in behind them. Villagers stared silently from doorways and windows as the soldiers passed. They looked afraid.

They turned a corner into a narrow alleyway between two shacks and followed it to a clearing behind the houses. A group of soldiers had surrounded a cluster of frightened-looking Malay villagers.

One of the soldiers stepped forward and saluted as Captain Hall approached.

"Well, Sergeant?" asked Captain Hall, returning the salute with a tired gesture.

"Bunch of fifth columnists, Captain," said the sergeant, pointing at the group of frightened men. "Remember those bombers that gave us a rough time as we approached the village? Well, now we know how they found us."

He stood back and pointed at a line of brightly coloured sarongs hanging from a makeshift clothes line. "These sods were signalling them!"

"Not true!" protested a skinny old man with a wispy white beard, his voice high. "We are friends of the British!"

"Rule Britannia!" croaked another Malay.

Captain Hall regarded them with cold eyes. "Sergeant, you know what to do with them," he said.

Olivia grabbed Captain Hall by the sleeve. "You can't do this!"

He looked down at her hand, then casually pulled his sleeve away.

"It's well known that the area is full of spies," he said. "Many of these people have been sympathetic to the Japanese for years. They've just been waiting for the chance to stab us in the back."

Olivia wouldn't listen to this rubbish. "You're British soldiers! These people are innocent. Leave them alone!"

He whirled on her and there was madness in his eyes. She'd seen it in the sergeant's, too. These were men who had reached their limit. "Listen to me, you brat! I lost three men less than an hour ago because, for some strange reason, a bunch of Japanese knew exactly where to drop their bombs!" He thrust a finger at the cowering villagers. "Because of these sods!"

"You can't . . ." Olivia's voice sounded hopelessly ineffectual, even to her.

"Sergeant! You have your orders! Carry them out . . . Now!"

Olivia and Georgia stumbled back up the alleyway with the sound of the villagers' crying ringing in their ears.

Out on the street Ho Lap stood as they had left him. Holding a suitcase in each hand, he looked like a tourist who had momentarily lost his way, but there was nothing leisurely about the two threatening soldiers who stood in front of him.

Olivia's body went cold.

"Leave him alone!" she shrieked.

Before she knew what she was doing, she was running full tilt at the soldiers. They turned at her cry and took a startled step backwards. Olivia skidded to a halt before them, her face full of anger. "You leave him alone!" she hissed.

The soldiers recovered from their initial shock. One of them gestured at Ho Lap.

"You know this bloke?"

"He's my houseb . . . He's my friend. My family has known him for years."

"Only he was acting pretty suspicious," the soldier continued. "There's a lot of spies about. We gotta be careful like."

"Oh, get lost!" snapped Georgia. She pushed past the soldiers and took her suitcase from Ho Lap's hand. "Come on, Ho Lap. Let's go."

"Hey!" protested the soldier.

"Why don't you go and find the real enemy instead of picking on innocent people?" said Olivia. Before the soldier could reply, she brushed past him, gently eased the other suitcase away from Ho Lap and set off down the road.

Her heart was thumping. She expected to be wrenched back with each step she took.

"Ah, let 'em go," she heard one of the soldiers say.

Rolling her eyes, she let out a sigh of relief and looked over at her companions. They met her gaze. And all three of them burst into tears.

None of them was in the mood to run into another English army patrol. So, rather than stick to the main road, they decided to follow the side track south, reasoning that it was bound to link up to the highway at some stage.

But it didn't. At least not that day.

Night fell with its customary suddenness and they were lucky to come across a deserted shack in which to shelter. It was little more than a lean-to, with gaping holes in the rotten timber walls, but it had a roof. When it started raining in the night, they were able to keep reasonably dry.

The last of the lunches was opened and shared with Ho Lap. He hunkered down on his haunches and chewed slowly. The night was so dark that Olivia could hardly see him, even though he was barely a metre away. But she didn't need to see him to sense his pain.

The rain drummed on the tin roof and the night wore on.

It was the cold that woke Olivia this time.

How she hated this jungle! Stifling in the day and freezing at night. At home, she was always able to haul up a blanket when the chill of the night descended, but out here there was no such luxury.

Her whole body was shaking. It didn't help that the clothes she was in were still damp with sweat.

She curled up into a ball and listened to Georgia's teeth chattering in the dark. At least I'm not the only one suffering, she thought with grim satisfaction.

Despite the cold, Olivia must have fallen asleep again for when she next opened her eyes it was daylight and the rain had stopped. Ho Lap was standing outside the shack. He turned when he heard the girls stir.

"We will have to do some swimming, I'm afraid," he said.

Well, at least he's talking again, thought Olivia. Maybe he's over what happened yesterday, she thought, without conviction. In his place, she wouldn't be.

She got up, her body stiff and sore – and filthy.

She'd never gone a day without showering. Now here she was with two days' worth of sweat and muck all over her. Finally, Ho Lap's words sank in. "What do you mean swim?"

Ho Lap pointed down the road. "The rains have swollen the river. There is a small bridge, but it is under water."

"You're joking!" Georgia got to her feet. "We've got to go back then!"

Ho Lap shook his head. "That would not be wise. The Japanese may not be far behind us. No. I tested the water while you were sleeping. It is not deep or flowing fast. I am confident that we can cross it."

The girls looked doubtfully at each other. "I dunno . . ." said Olivia.

Truth be told, she wasn't keen on the idea at all. She was a lousy swimmer. She could barely swim a non-stop length of the pool at her mother's club, so she didn't fancy her chances in a raging torrent.

"Come," said Ho Lap, picking up the suitcases and striding off. "I will show you."

"Haven't got a lot of choice, have we?" grumbled Georgia.

It was as bad as the girls had expected it to be. The mud road disappeared into a brown, swiftly flowing river.

"The bridge hasn't collapsed," explained Ho Lap. "It is merely submerged. I doubt that the water will rise above our waists. If we approach the crossing carefully, there should be no problems."

Olivia looked at him with disbelief. "You *are* joking, aren't you? We can't cross that!"

"We cannot stay here," said Ho Lap. "The Japanese will be here soon."

Olivia remembered his warning of the previous day. She wanted to scream! Stay here and face the Japanese or try and cross over and get drowned instead. What sort of choice was that?

"I will hold you," said Ho Lap. "You will be safe." He smiled. It was the first time Olivia had ever seen the man smile. It was warm and reassuring. "Trust me."

"Oh, come on!" said Georgia impatiently. "Here! I'll show you how easy it is!"

She made her way into the water and paused for a moment, gauging the force of the current. Then she turned side on to the flow and, with small, deliberate steps, began to edge her way across. The water soon reached above her knees and halfway up her thighs. Olivia watched with wide eyes, her heart thumping. Any moment now, she expected her friend to lose her footing and be swept away.

CHAPTER *three*

But Georgia stayed upright. The water swirled around her waist and continued to rise but, just past the halfway mark, the level of the water began to drop until finally she was splashing out on the other side. She turned and waved, a huge smile on her face. "Come on! It's easy!"

Still Olivia hesitated. It's all right for you, she thought. You're a born athlete.

Sensing her fear, Ho Lap suggested that he take the suitcases over and then come back for her.

Olivia watched while he picked up the suitcases and began to make his way across.

There was a noise in the jungle behind her – something big pushing through the foliage. The Japanese! In a panic, Olivia plunged into the river. Instead of walking slowly to keep her balance, she tried to run. And that proved her undoing.

The current caught at her legs and knocked them out from under her. She managed one short, shrill scream before her mouth filled with foul-tasting water. She flailed, trying to regain her feet, but the current had her now.

Her arms and legs thrashed uselessly and for one brief instant her head broke the surface. She had a blurred impression of brown and green and then she went under again.

She was rolling over and over now. Her head hit something hard. She opened her mouth to cry out and the water surged in.

Suddenly, a hand grabbed her under one arm and she was hauled to the surface. She felt herself being dragged against the current. A body pressed hard against hers. A voice shouted something at her, but she couldn't tell what it was saying. It sounded so far away.

The water was gone now. She was lying on hard ground. A shadow fell over her, fingers roughly prised her lips apart. Her head was being tilted backwards. Someone was breathing down her throat! Argh! That's disgusting! Now hands were pushing at her chest.

Water boiled up in her throat and gushed out her mouth. She coughed and spluttered and retched.

"She's okay!" Olivia recognised Georgia's voice. "She's okay! You saved her, Ho Lap."

She opened her eyes. Ho Lap was kneeling beside her. Behind him stood Georgia. Was she crying?

"I heard Japanese behind me," muttered Olivia.

Georgia's laugh came out as a splutter. "A wild pig is what you heard, you idiot!"

CHAPTER *three*

They reached the main highway a short time later. The sun had broken through the clouds and once again the jungle steamed in the heat.

The girls trudged on in their drenched gear. There wasn't any point in changing. All the clothing in their suitcases was soaked from the dunking in the river.

On they squelched. Now that the sky was clear once more, Japanese planes began to fly overhead. And once more the jungle was filled with the thump-thump-thump of distant explosions.

In the late afternoon, they reached a fork in the road. A large signpost pointed out destinations in four different directions. Ho Lap suggested that they rest for a while. He would drape their wet clothing over the arms of the signpost in an effort to dry them.

The jungle had given way to a rubber plantation, so the foliage wasn't as thick as before. The girls found themselves a reasonably clear spot in the shade just off the road and Georgia stretched out on her back. It wasn't long before she was snoring softly.

But Olivia's mind still buzzed from her close call with death. There was no way she was going to sleep – not for a while anyway. She hunkered down with her back against the trunk of a rubber tree and watched as Ho Lap carefully arranged the sodden garments over the signpost.

His movements were so dainty. Almost like a woman's.

As Olivia watched this quiet little man, with his bald head and sticky-out ears, she felt a glow in the pit of her stomach. You've always been there for me, she thought. More than my parents, that's for sure.

Whenever I was hungry, who gave me my meals? Whenever I fell and cut my knee or banged my head, who was there to nurse me and tell me everything was going to be all right? When Lana and her cronies gave me a rough time once at school, who came to pick me up?

You. It was always you.

Never Mother, thought Olivia, shocked at the bitterness she suddenly felt. When she thought about it, her mother had never been there. Not when it counted. Always down at the club or entertaining friends. Like now. She's in Singapore, enjoying the high life probably, while I'm running for my life and Dad is . . . Olivia didn't want to think about that any more.

Her thoughts drifted back to Ho Lap. It surprised her – how much she had always taken him for granted. When her mother said that Ho Lap was just doing his job and that, if they stopped paying him, he'd move on, she had believed her. How stupid!

It was more than a job for you, wasn't it, Ho Lap? You put up with so much rubbish from our family. Okay, we weren't mean to you (well, Mother might have come pretty close). But we weren't exactly nice. I don't think I ever thanked you. Not once.

Employees wouldn't put up with that sort of thing. She remembered some of the foremen Dad had employed. Big, burly Dutch guys. One wrong word and they were off like a shot, giving Dad an earful before they went.

But not Ho Lap. Or his wife. They had always been there. And now he was risking his life for her. No, her mother had been wrong. Ho Lap was more than a servant. Much more.

Her eyelids began to grow heavy. "Ho Lap." Her voice was a tired croak.

Ho Lap paused in his work and looked around.

"Thank you," said Olivia.

Ho Lap smiled that beautiful, warm smile again. Olivia's eyelids drooped and as she fell asleep she thought of Ho Lap's daughter. *I wonder how old she was when she died?*

CHAPTER *four*

Olivia came awake with a start. What was that? It sounded like a shot. The Japanese! Then she heard voices. English voices.

"Georgia!" she whispered, and realised that her friend was standing up, staring at something on the road. She had a strange expression on her face.

"What . . . ?"

Olivia got up and followed her friend's gaze. Her heart stopped.

Ho Lap lay on his back next to the signpost, one of Olivia's blouses clutched in his hands. Five English soldiers stood in a semicircle around him. One of them held a pistol loosely by his side. A wisp of smoke drifted from the barrel.

There was a strange high-pitched ringing in Olivia's ears and her vision seemed to narrow in on the English soldier with the smoking pistol.

She heard a savage growl. She didn't realise it was coming from her.

She marched forward. The soldiers looked up, finally aware of her presence.

"You killed him," roared Olivia.

Confused, the soldier with the gun looked towards his comrades, but they were backing away. Olivia didn't care. They meant nothing to her. Nothing did, except the soldier with the gun.

"He was my friend."

The soldier looked at the pistol in his hand as if he didn't know how it had got there. "I thought he was a spy," he squeaked. "I thought he was signalling Japanese airplanes with those clothes."

"He was my friend."

"I didn't know . . ."

Olivia was almost on the soldier now. He tried to retreat, but Olivia punched him in the nose with all her might.

The soldier shrieked. Blood, red and bright, squirted across his face. "She broke by dose!" he wailed.

"Little savages!" the soldiers said.

"She broke by dose!" the injured soldier wailed again.

"So what do we do with 'em?"

"Give 'em a bleedin' good hiding, if you ask me."

"Oh yeah! The big man!" It was Georgia, her voice dripping with contempt. "Shoot an unarmed civilian and whip a couple of teenage girls. Your mums must be really proud of you!"

"Oi! What is going on here?"

It was a woman's voice. Loud and strong, with an Australian accent.

None of them had heard two army lorries rumble to a halt nearby. They had big white circles with red crosses painted on the sides.

A tall woman with raven black hair showing beneath her wide-brimmed hat stormed towards the group of soldiers. She was dressed in a white blouse, a khaki skirt and no-nonsense brown shoes. A sash on her arm, depicting a bright red cross, stood out against the drabness of the clothing. The uniform may have been pristine once, but heat and rain had done their work and it was now covered in mud, hanging like a badly made bed.

She was the kind of woman Olivia's mother would have called handsome rather than beautiful. On a good day, that face would probably have guys offering her flowers. But, right now, it was set in an expression of fury that would make the strongest man quail.

The soldiers seemed to shrink with every step she took towards them. "Which one of you clowns is in charge here?"

The soldier with the broken nose raised his hand. "She broke by dose," he squeaked pathetically.

"She broke my nose, *sir*! I'm a captain, soldier!"

The nurse stood before them, hands on hips. "So what happened here?" She noticed for the first time the body of Ho Lap lying on the road. "Who's he?"

"Our friend!" Olivia blurted. "They murdered him!"

The reference to murder made several of the soldiers pale. "Now hold on one second," one of them said quickly. "We saw him hanging out all those clothes over there. We thought he was signalling to Japanese planes." He fixed the nurse with a pleading look. "You've heard the stories about fifth columnists being as thick as fleas around 'ere."

The corner of the nurse's mouth curled up. "Yep. I've heard the stories. Load of rubbish, if you ask me. So you killed an innocent man because he was hanging out washing?"

"On a signpost!" protested the soldier.

"Our clothes got wet when we were crossing a river back there," explained Georgia calmly. Olivia was impressed. Her own fury at the soldiers had made her speechless. "Ho Lap was hanging them out to dry while we slept. I guess these idiots didn't even give him a chance to explain. They just . . . shot him." Her voice faltered.

The soldiers looked at each other silently. The heat of the moment had gone. Now only the shame remained.

Tears poured down Olivia's face. She thought of Ho Lap and his wife whispering and embracing on the veranda. Of the terrible way in which he drove her father's car, all graunching gears and jerking movements. And of that beautiful smile that had followed her into sleep. Now he was dead.

The nurse saw her tears and her features softened. She put an arm around Olivia's shoulders.

"Let it out, hon," she said, her voice quiet and soothing. "Don't worry. Just let it out." She turned to Georgia. "Where were you headed before . . . ?"

"Kuala Krai," replied Georgia, her voice still shaky. She quickly recapped the events of the last few days.

"Well, that's where we're going," said the nurse. "You can come with us." She turned to the soldiers who stood in shamefaced misery. "As for you lot, I want this man buried. Decently, mind."

They nodded.

"I want to stay while they bury him," pleaded Olivia.

"I'm sorry, hon," said the nurse quietly, giving Olivia a reassuring squeeze. "There are a lot of seriously wounded soldiers in the back of those trucks. We need to get them to the train so they can get to a decent hospital. There's nothing more you can do for Ho Lap. But those boys in the trucks over there can still make it if we hurry."

She turned and strode back to the trucks with the girls trailing after her.

As they reached the vehicles, the nurse clapped her hand to her forehead. "Strewth!" she exclaimed, with a force that made the girls jump. "Where are my manners?" She thrust out a hand. "I'm Ida Wright of the Australian Army Nursing Corps." She nodded towards the sullen group of English soldiers. "Those goons over there call me Captain, but you can call me Ida." She gave the girls a conspiratorial wink.

Olivia looked back at the soldiers surrounding the crumpled body of Ho Lap and felt the tears rising again. She tore her eyes away.

"Right then. Let's find you some room. We're a bit tight, I'm afraid. But I'm sure we'll manage." She led Olivia and Georgia around to the back of the truck and lifted the canvas flap. "You'll have to ride back here. Don't worry. They won't bite. Will you, lads?"

There were a few guffaws, then someone started coughing. It sounded wet and painful, as if he was hawking up his insides.

The sound disconcerted the girls and they hesitated. "Come on now," said Ida gently. "We've got to get cracking."

When the girls climbed into the dim interior, the smell told them what to expect long before their eyes adjusted to the lack of light. The coppery stench of blood was mixed with the horrible antiseptic smell Olivia remembered from her visit to the hospital at Kota Baharu.

The man was still coughing. He was lying on a stretcher set against the side of the truck, his entire torso swathed in bandages. A nurse knelt next to him, mopping his brow with a wet rag and making soft, soothing noises.

On the other side of the truck, six men sat in a row. All of them wore bandages. One had his arm in a sling. Another had his head wrapped up so completely, he looked like the invisible man. His head jerked around with every sound.

The truck lurched into motion. One of the men fell sideways and uttered a curse. Olivia blushed.

"Language, Sam!" the nurse scolded gently.

"Well, tell that bleedin' driver to watch what he's doing!" Sam retorted, unrepentant. "Crikey! I could do a better job than he is and I've only got one arm!"

The girls sat pressed against the tailgate, eyeing the injured men warily.

The truck rattled on, raising a chorus of groans and curses with every bump it hit. The second truck followed close behind.

Maybe they'll know about Dad, thought Olivia. I've got to ask. Like Ida said, they're not going to bite. "Was anyone here at Kota Baharu?" she blurted.

All eyes turned to her. She swallowed.

"Bleedin' shambles," the one called Sam muttered at last. "We had 'em on the beaches good and proper. We could have kept 'em there, too. But the flyboys let us down."

"What happened?" coaxed Olivia after a few seconds of silence.

Sam looked at her. "Like I said, the Aussie air force dropped us in it. They just stopped showing up. Next thing we know, the Japanese have landed a whole bunch more soldiers and the place is teeming with 'em. Would have been a different story if the bleedin' Aussie air force had stuck around."

At that moment, the truck behind them exploded in a ball of flame.

"No!" shouted someone, as the blazing wreck careened across the road and smashed into the jungle.

Olivia looked up to see a Japanese fighter plane sweeping towards them. Little flashes of light winked along the plane's wings. Bullets tore through the canvas roof. There were screams and the world began to tumble over and over . . .

Olivia opened her eyes. Her head hurt. She raised her hand to her temple and winced as she felt a lump there. It felt like the size of a tennis ball.

She eased herself up and found she was sitting on the side of the road. There was an insistent crackling sound and the smell of smoke. The truck she had been travelling in lay on its side twenty metres away with flames licking from its open bonnet. Figures lay sprawled and twisted around the wrecked vehicle.

Still dazed, Olivia managed to get to her feet. She felt giddy for a second, but after a moment the world returned to normal.

"You okay?" Georgia came up beside her. One of the arms of her blouse had been torn away and there were streaks of blood on her upper arm. She rubbed at it absent-mindedly.

Olivia nodded. "Just a bit of a headache. What . . . "

"Japanese fighters." Olivia turned and noticed Ida sitting next to two bodies in the shade of a palm tree. Olivia walked over. As she came closer, she was surprised to see that the two figures on the ground were still alive, but one look at Ida's expression told her they weren't going to be that way for much longer.

One of them was the young nurse from the back of the truck. She lay quite still, her blue eyes staring up at something that only she could see.

The other figure lay with his legs twisted at a weird angle. It was Sam. He was holding on to Ida's hand, his knuckles white with the effort.

"Funny," he said, a strained smile showing beneath the blood on his lips. "Come all the way from Yorkshire just to die in a stinkin' hot country like this."

Ida patted his hand.

"Ah well, at least I've seen a bit of the world," Sam went on philosophically. "Not like me old man. I think the furthest he got was London." He winced as pain shot through his body, then fell silent, looking up at the trees above him.

"Did anyone else . . . ?" Olivia asked.

Ida shook her head. "You've got to get away from here. The Japanese could be here at any time."

Olivia looked at Sam and the nurse. "But how can we carry . . ."

Ida didn't let her finish. "We're staying here."

Olivia was confused. "What do you mean?"

"I'm not leaving them alone. They need someone to be with them."

"But you said yourself the Japanese could be here any moment now."

"They won't hurt me," replied Ida. "I'm a nurse."

That didn't stop them shooting up the Red Cross trucks, thought Olivia. "Maybe we can use one of the stretchers from the trucks?" she suggested.

"No." Ida looked down at the injured. "We couldn't move them even if we wanted to. And besides, if we tried, they'd die."

"They're going to die anyway!" Olivia flushed with shame as soon as the words left her mouth. But neither Sam nor the nurse seemed to hear her. They both had faraway looks in their eyes now.

"I know," said Ida. "And I'll be with them when they do. But you two." She pointed down the road. "You've got to get to Kuala Krai. Your fathers didn't send you away so you could get captured on some jungle road. Go! Now!"

She had the same expression she had worn when she confronted the English soldiers. And, like those soldiers, Olivia and Georgia wilted beneath her glare. There would be no further argument.

"Good luck," said Olivia. It sounded so feeble.

But it seemed to be enough for Ida. She smiled. "You, too," she said softly.

And so they set off to Kuala Krai. It didn't seem right, deserting the person who had helped them. But they went anyway. Olivia looked back only once. Ida was saying something to Sam and stroking his head. He was still holding her hand.

Kuala Krai was a ghost town. When the girls reached the railway station, they could see the main street of the market town behind it. There was no sign of life. The station was equally deserted.

A heavy silence hung over everything. The girls climbed the concrete steps onto the wide station platform. The soft padding of their feet sounded incredibly loud.

They stood there, looking up and down the track. No train. No people. Nothing.

"You'll not find any of your countrymen here." A man emerged from the dark interior of the station house. He was an Indian, tall and thin and dressed completely in white. His white shirt was neatly pressed, with large damp patches beneath his arms. The white trousers were also neatly creased. He even wore white shoes. What a pain they must be to keep clean, thought Olivia.

On his head, the man wore a white trilby that kept half his face in shadow even as he came into the sunlight. He carried himself erect, but walked with a halting stride, supporting his left leg with a thick wooden cane. He leaned on it as he came to a halt in front of the girls.

"I am Dr Sidhu," he said, touching the brim of his hat and making a slight bow in greeting. "I have a dental practice in this town." There was a hint of pride as he mentioned his profession.

"Where is everyone?" asked Georgia, continuing to scan the deserted station and the silent town beyond.

"Oh, there are still people here," said Dr Sidhu, following her gaze. "But none of your people. Not any more."

"What are you talking about?" snapped Georgia impatiently, suddenly annoyed at Dr Sidhu's mysterious air. She'd been through enough without having to decipher what this man was saying.

CHAPTER *four*

"Oh, I'm sorry," replied Dr Sidhu, in a tone that indicated that he was not sorry at all. "Am I not being clear enough for you? All of the Europeans fled yesterday. They took the last train out." He paused. "They would not permit any of us to go with them."

His tone had grown ugly. He removed his hat and wiped his brow with the back of his forearm. His hair, like the rest of him, was neat, parted smartly down the middle. The Brylcreem he used to keep his hair in place gleamed in the sun. There was a touch of grey at his temples.

He continued. "Whites only, they said. The soldiers beat us back with clubs. Even the women and children. Even them."

"What a load of rubbish!" spat Georgia. But Olivia wasn't so sure. Not after what she'd seen in the last few days.

Dr Sidhu tilted his head slightly. "Believe what you will. But I speak the truth."

"But why?" asked Olivia. "Why would they do that?"

Dr Sidhu fixed her with his stare. "Because they were frightened. The day before yesterday, we heard the news that your mighty warships, the *Prince of Wales* and *Repulse*, were sunk by the Japanese." He smiled. "I think you British set great store by those ships. Then we heard that the Japanese had taken Kota Baharu and were coming down the peninsula. That, as you British say, was the last straw."

"We're *not* British!" retorted Georgia. "I'm from Australia, actually."

"Australian? Ah yes. Like us, you are part of the great British Empire." Dr Sidhu's eyes narrowed. "But where is the mighty empire now?"

Olivia tried to meet the man's stare but couldn't.

Georgia just snorted. "The Japanese may have the upper hand now. But we'll show 'em."

To Olivia's surprise, Dr Sidhu agreed. "I dare say you're right. After all, you have the Americans on your side. But I think that, even if you win the war, you will lose your empire. I think the people here will see that their great white gods have feet of clay. You will not be welcome back here."

Olivia said nothing.

"So there's no train then," said Georgia. "Is that what you're saying?"

Dr Sidhu shifted his cane slightly. Clearly, standing in the same spot for so long caused him discomfort. But Olivia could see from the pride in his eyes that he wasn't going to admit it.

"Where are you headed?" he asked, changing the

subject. He spoke as if his earlier tirade hadn't even happened.

"Singapore," replied Olivia.

"Ah, Singapore. The island fortress with its mighty guns." Again, his voice took on a sarcastic tone and again he fixed Olivia with a searching stare. "Do you think you will be safe there?"

Olivia shrugged. "Safer than here, anyway."

Dr Sidhu pulled a face. "Perhaps. But Singapore is a long way away. How do you intend getting there, now that there is no train?"

"We'll walk!" said Georgia defiantly.

Dr Sidhu regarded her for a few seconds. Unlike Olivia, Georgia met his gaze full on and held it.

Finally, the doctor smiled. "I'm sure you will. And you'll probably make it, too. You have that determined look about you. Like the fabled English bulldog, eh?"

And then, as if suddenly tired of their company, he turned on his heel and began to walk towards the silent town. "I hope that Singapore does not fall before you get there," he called back carelessly.

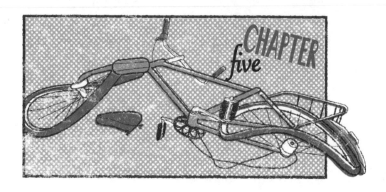

CHAPTER five

The two girls wandered along the cracked white road in silence, lost in their own thoughts. Around them the jungle chirruped and squawked. Night fell and they slept by the verge, too tired to worry about looking for any form of shelter. When it got cold, they simply huddled together for warmth.

They were awake before dawn and resumed their journey on empty, aching stomachs. Olivia thought back on the boiled eggs and crisp toast that Ho Lap prepared for her every morning.

Poor Ho Lap. He'd been with her family for years, yet she'd only really started to know him in his final day of life.

Another day passed. And another.

They walked in that brief cool time before night became day. Then the sun rose and brought with it the stifling heat that had become their constant companion. Their canteens of water were soon empty.

"We'd better come across someone soon," said Georgia, "or they're gonna find us lying here with our tongues all purple and hanging out."

On and on they trudged. A dull, throbbing pain started in the backs of Olivia's legs and slowly crept over her entire body, so that her only reality was pain.

"Where the heck is everyone?" moaned Georgia.

Dr Sidhu was right. Everyone had fled south.

They came across a tin mine. Perhaps there was someone here! They raced down the dirt road to the homestead, but a thick column of black smoke told them there was no hope to be had there. They ran on anyway – they didn't really know why, they just didn't know what else to do.

The smoke was coming from the mining equipment. Someone had doused it in petrol and set it alight. It must have been blazing for some time, because the flames were low now and the equipment already twisted into grotesque shapes by the intense heat.

"Japanese!" Georgia looked around, as if expecting to see hordes of Japanese soldiers appear around them. But somehow Olivia doubted that the

Japanese had done this. The destruction seemed too planned. Could the owners have done it themselves before fleeing?

The homestead was still intact, as if the occupants expected to return and rebuild their livelihood.

"Let's look through the house," said Olivia. "There could be food and water in there."

The front door was locked, so Georgia simply smashed one of the windows in. Olivia was beyond being shocked. Besides, she was starving. And they needed whatever was in there more than the people who had left it.

They found some bread and several cans of tinned fruit. Everything else was gone. Georgia tracked down a can opener and they attacked the food with gusto, then rummaged around for a bag in which to carry the few extra cans.

They were heading down the hallway with their loot when Georgia spied something in the living room.

"What is it?" asked Olivia, following her into the room. The sun was setting, throwing deep shadows across the floor, and the house that had seemed so warm and inviting now had a sinister air about it. She felt a shiver tickle her spine.

Georgia was standing by a piano on the far side

of the room, looking at something in her hand. As Olivia approached, she saw that it was a framed photograph. A man and a woman with a young girl beamed out at them from a happier time.

"Must be the family who lived here," said Olivia. She glanced at her friend and was shocked to see that her eyes were glistening.

"I miss my mum and dad," said Georgia, after a moment's silence. Her attention was still focused on the photograph.

Olivia felt a lump rise in her throat. "Me, too," she croaked.

Georgia smiled, but there was sadness behind it. "Remember how Mum always took us to the beach?"

Olivia nodded. They were great days, full of sunshine and promise.

"And when Mum and Dad used to take us up to that resort in the high country when the weather got too hot. It was so lovely up there."

Olivia remembered, and with it came a pang of envy as she realised that she had probably seen more of Georgia's parents than her own. Maybe that wasn't really true, but it felt that way.

Georgia's mother was so different from Olivia's. So much so that sometimes Olivia wondered why the two were such firm friends. Georgia's mother always seemed to be there. She was never off at the club. Olivia often heard her refer to the club members as a pack of sour old prunes. And, even though they had servants, whenever Olivia was visiting it was always Georgia's mother who prepared the meals and took them on jaunts to the beach or to the shops in town.

"Do you think they're still alive?"

The question jerked Olivia away from her thoughts. "What?"

"What if the Japanese have taken Singapore? They could have, you know."

"Nahhh," said Olivia, with more confidence than she felt. "They couldn't have got that far."

Georgia shrugged. Her attention returned to the photograph and she lapsed into silence once more.

Olivia watched her friend. She'd never seen her like this before. It made her nervous.

With a sudden movement that made Olivia jump, Georgia placed the photo back on top of the piano. "Let's get out of here," she said.

They walked through the twilight and on into the night. Neither of them said anything, but they wanted to put as much distance as possible between themselves and that house and all the memories it had conjured up.

Sunrise found them still plodding along on tired legs. Exhaustion had numbed them beyond all feeling.

Singapore. That was all that mattered now.

By late morning, they had reached and crossed a wooden bridge straddling a murky brown river. A little further ahead, the road disappeared around a bend. They had just reached it when they heard a strange clickety-clack sound behind them. Voices, too. Only they weren't speaking English.

"Japanese!" hissed Georgia, looking back the way they had come.

This time Olivia was inclined to agree with her. The road behind them was empty. But the clickety-clack sound and the voices were getting closer.

"Sounds like a lot of 'em!" said Georgia. "Come on! Let's get out of here!"

They started to run down the road.

"Hold it!" panted Olivia. "This is dumb. If we carry on along the road, they're bound to catch up. Let's hide in the jungle until they've passed us."

They threw themselves off the road and barged into the thick undergrowth. For a brief instant, Olivia's world was a mass of green. And then her foot struck something soft and she went flying.

She heard a yelp of pain.

"Watch where you're going, you stupid cow!"

She raised herself up on her arms. A scrawny, pale-faced soldier glared at her from under a round steel helmet that was far too big for him, lending him an awkward, gawky look. He was lying flat on his stomach, rubbing his side where Olivia's foot had caught him.

Georgia stood over him. "Who are you calling a stupid cow, you creep!"

Now we're for it, thought Olivia. But, instead of getting up, the soldier started to tug at the hem of Georgia's skirt. "Shut up and get down!" he hissed. He had the same accent as Georgia. An Australian!

Georgia bristled. "Don't tell me to shut up!"

The soldier spat back, still tugging madly. "Both of you shut your traps."

Olivia turned to the source of a growling sound. A burly man was glowering at them from behind the trunk of a fallen tree. Like the soldier they had tripped over, he wore a steel helmet, but his seemed to fit him a lot better. Olivia could see the stubby barrel of a machine-gun sticking up beside him.

He gestured impatiently for them to lie down.

It was then that Olivia realised that the jungle

around them was alive with soldiers. They were all lying silently amid the foliage, their heads raised, peering intently at the road like a herd of curious lizards.

They must have reached the Australian army! They were safe!

This was a deadly-looking bunch, though, with faces like leather, cradling guns of various sorts. Olivia recognised some rifles, but there were other weapons she had never seen before – wicked, heavy-looking things with long barrels and funny curved pieces sticking out of the top. They were so big, they needed to be supported by little tripods at the end of the barrel.

Beside each soldier lay heaps of what looked like small black pineapples with rings at the top.

The burly man hissed and gestured again, more emphatically this time, and Olivia and Georgia sank quietly down until they were lying flat on the evil-smelling earth.

The strange click-clacking sound and the carefree chatter of the Japanese soldiers were louder now. They must be almost in front of them. No wonder the guy behind the tree was so furious.

Olivia looked across at the soldier she had tripped over. He was so close, she could see the sweat rolling down the side of his face and the nervous twitch of his mouth.

He's as frightened as I am, she thought. He's acting like the big man, but he's terrified.

She noticed the pale fluff growing on his jowls. He didn't even shave yet. He couldn't be much older than her. Yet here he was, lying in the muck with a gun, fighting in a war that made no sense. He should be at school. Or having fun with his mates at the beach.

It wasn't right. Nothing was right any more.

The noise on the road was incredibly loud now. It sounded as if there were hundreds of men out there. Thousands even. A great mass of men on bicycles. So that's what the click-clacking sound had been.

They swarmed past, laughing and talking as if they were out on a Sunday jaunt. So this was the Japanese army. They didn't look anything like she'd expected them to – not like an army of conquerors anyway. They seemed almost . . . normal. Some wore army shirts, but many were dressed in white skivvies and others didn't have any shirts on at all. Their khaki trousers hung loose, cinched tight at the knee by puttees or leggings.

Some of the riders yelled something at a soldier who had dismounted to adjust his bike chain – it was obviously some good-natured badgering because he waved his fist at them and then laughed.

He's so young, she thought. Why is it that all the soldiers seem to be so young?

On and on the great army of cyclists came. None of them looked ready for a fight.

Olivia glanced over at the long row of Australians lying in the dim light of the jungle, then at the unsuspecting riders. It was going to be a massacre.

I should feel glad, she thought, after all the Japanese have done to us. But she didn't. She didn't know what she felt.

She looked back at the road and a terrible chill raced down her spine. The Japanese soldier who had been fiddling with his bike was looking directly at her. A puzzled smile crossed his face. He looked as if he was about to say something, then Olivia felt the ground heave beneath her. A great roar seemed to roll towards her like an express train.

The Japanese soldiers stopped and looked behind them. A strange stillness fell across the road as if the world had paused to take a breath.

"That's the bridge gone!" someone shouted from behind Olivia. "No way back for the beggars now!"

The jungle erupted with the sound of gunfire. Machine-guns rattled, rifles cracked.

Olivia looked away. Maybe if she didn't watch, she wouldn't hear the screams.

She heard the crump-crump-crump of explosions. Some strange impulse made her lift her head to look at the road, though she had no wish to see what was happening there.

She felt a hand press firmly down on her head. "Get your head down unless you want it blown off," shouted the burly soldier. To make sure she didn't get up, he knelt on Olivia's back. The breath whooshed out of her and she breathed in a mouthful of foul-tasting muck. She tried to wriggle out from beneath him, but he pushed down harder.

"Stay put!" he growled.

Olivia lay there for what seemed like an eternity, trying to breathe without taking in any more mud. There were screams everywhere now.

Georgia! She looked around for her friend and saw her wink at her from a mud-covered face.

The firing went on. The explosions became so frequent that they became one overwhelming noise.

And then suddenly it was over.

The burly soldier looked down at Olivia.

"You can get up now, miss," he said, his voice strangely soft and kind now the battle was over. "Up you get, Dave," he said, giving the scrawny young soldier a gentle nudge in the ribs. The boy winced.

The Australian soldiers emerged from the jungle, hundreds of them, and began moving among the carpet of dead and wounded Japanese.

A thin blue haze of smoke hung low over the scene, giving the soldiers a surreal look, as if they were part of a nightmare.

"What do we do with the wounded, sir?" one of the men asked.

"Let their own medics sort 'em out," replied a tall, broad-shouldered man who looked a little older than the rest. "We can't take 'em with us. Okay, lads! Check for any documents they may be carrying. Go for the officers first. And hurry it up. We don't want to hang around here any longer than we need to."

Olivia was stunned. "You can't leave them out here in the sun. They'll die!"

The officer glanced quickly in her direction, then carried on as if she hadn't spoken. As Olivia felt the rage boil within her, a hand fell on her shoulder and squeezed it gently.

"The major's right," said the burly soldier kindly. "We couldn't take them with us even if we wanted to. No room in the trucks, see. And if we hang around here much longer the Japanese'll be all over us."

"But . . ."

"Come on, luv," he said, smiling the warm smile that seemed so strange on those weathered features. The image of her father sprang into her mind and Olivia suddenly felt very tired. Too tired to argue about anything she had no control over.

Olivia and Georgia were crammed into the back of a lorry with a dozen soldiers. Unlike the Red Cross truck, this one was open to the elements. A hot wind covered Olivia with a fine dust and dried the sweat on her face. She felt clammy and filthy. Oh, what she'd give for a bath.

The men around her – all weathered, unshaven skin and lank, greasy hair – looked as filthy as she felt. Their dank-smelling, uncomfortable-looking uniforms hung on them. Some scratched at lice and other tiny bugs that had made themselves at home on their unwashed bodies.

Every now and then, Olivia caught a waft of the stench of the man sitting next to her. Maybe being in an open-air truck wasn't so bad after all. She felt something bite at her stomach. Oh no. She scratched furiously and it felt better. For the moment anyway.

They were part of a huge convoy. Trucks stretched in front of them as far as they could see, brimming with soldiers. Others were stretched out behind them – a great, long line disappearing into the billowing dust thrown up by the column.

At any other time, the sight of so much power would have impressed Olivia. Filled her with hope. But these men were on the run. And the thought made her feel more depressed than ever. If these guys were retreating, what hope did her father have?

No, can't think that way. He got out. I know he did. And Georgia's dad, too. And Ho Lap's wife. They all got out. They had to.

She felt Georgia nudge her in the ribs and looked over to see her nodding at something opposite them. "Looks like you've got a secret admirer." Her voice was filled with mischief.

Dave sat opposite them, staring at Olivia. He wasn't even trying to be subtle about it. He just stared, his grey eyes boring into her. Olivia squirmed uncomfortably under his silent gaze.

Finally, she couldn't stand it any longer. "What?" she barked.

Dave fidgeted, opening and closing his mouth as if the words would come out of their own accord. At last he managed to speak. "I just wanna say . . ." He ran out of steam.

Olivia leaned towards him a little. "Yes? You

wanna say . . . ?"

"I wanna say I'm sorry for calling you a stupid cow back there." He blushed and looked away.

Some of the men in the truck began to snicker.

Olivia could see that Dave was deeply embarrassed in front of his mates and she felt a sudden urge to jump to his rescue. "You seem awfully young to be in the army," she said, attempting to change the subject. But that only made it worse.

"I'm eighteen!" he cried indignantly.

Olivia didn't say anything. Now it was her turn to stare. His resolve melted under her scrutiny. "Well," he muttered, "I'm almost eighteen."

The hatchet-faced soldier sitting next to him burst out laughing and slapped the boy hard on the back. "Nothing to be ashamed of, son," he said. "I know a few lads who lied about their age to get into the army. And you did all right back there."

"Too right," said another. "Considering it was your first scrap and all."

Dave seemed to grow as the compliments flew, his anger and embarrassment quickly forgotten.

And then the bombers came.

CHAPTER *five*

The first they knew about it was a string of massive explosions in the jungle alongside the road that showered them with dirt and foliage. The driver swerved as a tall tree, sliced in half by the blast, toppled onto the road in front of them.

Men cried out and the truck behind disappeared in a ball of flame. As Olivia felt the blast of hot air against her face, the charred ruin of the cab flew through the air and crashed into the undergrowth. The next truck in the convoy ploughed into what was left of the blazing wreck and Olivia watched as men tumbled out of the back and threw themselves flat onto the road.

Another series of blasts rent the ground around them, but their own truck continued to weave along the road, throwing its passengers this way and that. Someone's flailing hand smacked Olivia in the nose and tears of pain sprang to her eyes.

And then it was over.

The truck screeched to a halt. Around them, the jungle looked as if a giant hand had pulled out great chunks of vegetation and scattered them about in a mindless frenzy. The road in front and behind was littered with blazing vehicles and human wreckage. Soldiers and men with red crosses on their armbands drifted in and out of the smoke, helping those who could still be helped and gently placing twisted helmets over the faces of those who couldn't. There were so few to help, Olivia thought, and so many bodies.

It was decided that staying put even for a few hours was too risky. To help reduce the threat of air attack, the major ordered that what was left of the convoy be split into three groups, with a twenty-minute gap between each. The truck that Olivia and Georgia were in was part of the second convoy.

Twenty minutes after the first convoy had disappeared around the bend, the second one set off. It was no longer a mighty fleet, but a bedraggled collection of ten trucks, filled with despairing, hollow-eyed men. Even Dave seemed to have aged ten years, Olivia noticed. He had a haunted look about him.

"Where are our glorious flyboys then?" somebody asked bitterly.

"The RAF?" Hatchet Face snorted. "You know what that stands for, don't you? Rare As Fairies."

A few of the men managed a grim laugh and looked up at the clear blue sky with worried eyes.

"I wish it would rain," croaked Dave.

CHAPTER *five*

But it didn't. And so, for the rest of that day and all of the next, the bombers came and went as the tiny fleet zigzagged along the road in a desperate effort to avoid being hit. They lost two trucks the first day, three more the next and they passed the wrecks of several other trucks. The first convoy had obviously suffered just as badly.

They passed through several small market towns. Only a few buildings had been hit by bombs, but the towns were devoid of any life. Deserted buildings threw back the echo of the trucks' engines. It was a flat, lonely sound, adding to the sense of desolation.

Olivia hated going through those towns. It was as if she was passing through the land of the dead, even though there wasn't a body in sight.

"Where is everyone?" Olivia asked no one in particular.

"Scarpered," explained the burly soldier, who was now sharing their truck. "And not necessarily because of the Japanese, either." He pointed to a pillar of black smoke coiling up behind a screen of trees. Olivia had noticed that these dark columns were becoming increasingly common the further south they travelled. "See that?"

Olivia nodded.

"My guess is it's the local tin mine. All the owners have been given orders to destroy their mines so the Japanese can't use 'em. They either blow 'em up or flood 'em, or both. Pretty good idea, too," he said. "Considering the Japanese need raw materials for their industry. They haven't got it in their own land, see. That's why they keep invading other countries."

"Since when did you get to know so much?" It was Hatchet Face. Olivia could tell he wasn't very impressed by the burly soldier's speech.

The soldier smiled at the interruption. "I was a school teacher back home. I taught social studies. As I was saying," he went on. "Depriving the Japanese of raw materials may make sound strategic sense, but it's not much good for the locals. The entire economy of these small towns is based around their local tin mines and plantations. With them gone, the town will just wither and die. So everyone's packed up and headed for Singapore."

"Ah, what a lot of rot," retorted Hatchet Face. "They've taken off because they know the Japanese will make their lives hell. That's why."

The burly soldier nodded. "I can't deny that. All Japan's talk about Asia being for the Asians and how everyone should stick together to throw the Europeans out doesn't quite hold water when you think about what they've been doing to the Chinese for the last few years. A lot of the locals will have left because of that." He paused and scratched his chin. "But not all. If the tin mines were going, you'd still see some people left in the towns, believe me."

"Do you think Dad destroyed our rubber plantation?" whispered Georgia.

Olivia shrugged.

"But what if he did? And your dad, too? I mean, if they were ordered to, they'd do it, right?"

"I guess." Olivia didn't want to dwell on it, as if just thinking about it would make it real.

"We won't have anything to go back to," said Georgia. For the first time since she'd known her friend, Olivia heard a note of uncertainty in her voice. In some strange way, that sign of weakness made her feel stronger.

On the third day, they caught up with the refugees. A huge procession of human misery clogged the road. Thousands of them – men, women, young and old. They were crammed into rickety old buses and trucks. Others rode along in bullock carts, pulled by great white beasts, many with children and old people perched on their backs.

The ones with some kind of transport, no matter how primitive, were the lucky ones. Most of the refugees were travelling on foot, some pulling rickshaws piled high with belongings. The convoy drivers blared their horns to clear the road, but no one moved out of the way.

The convoy's pace slowed down to that of the refugees.

When the planes came, everyone bolted for the meagre protection of the jungle, soldiers along with civilians, for there was no question of the trucks being able to zigzag between the hail of bombs now.

After the bombs stopped falling, everyone returned wraithlike to the road and resumed their trek. Some wailed, mourning a loved one. Wounded men, women and children staggered along and those who couldn't walk lay on the side of the road.

Sometimes the medics offered them aid, but there were too many. And the Japanese planes might return at any moment. So the tiny fleet of trucks pushed through the crowd and the people suffered.

It went on like that for two more days. No one talked any more. Dave sat silent and sullen. The burly soldier and Hatchet Face had faraway looks in their eyes, as if searching for somewhere better than here. Even Georgia's usual boisterous spirits had been reduced to silence.

They had been travelling for five days when Olivia spied an enormous cloud of black smoke hovering in the distance. It wasn't like the smoke from the burning tin mines. This was huge. It hung over the landscape like a malevolent force of nature.

"What's that?" asked Olivia.

The burly soldier looked at it briefly. When he spoke it was in a tired, flat tone. "That's Singapore."

The city of Singapore is on the south end of an island located at the bottom of the Malay peninsula. As the remnants of the convoy passed over the wide concrete causeway that connected the island to the mainland, Olivia saw soldiers busy at work connecting wires to square brown objects fixed to the sides of the bridge.

"They're rigging the bridge to blow," said Hatchet Face, craning to see. "That's not good."

Olivia shot the burly soldier a questioning look. He had the look of someone who had just been told news that confirmed his worst fears. "They've given up on Malaya," he explained. "They're going to blow the bridge and make their stand here on the island."

Olivia felt a chill. What about Dad?

They had reached the island by now. The coastline

stretched away from them on both sides of the road and all along it Olivia could see soldiers digging slit trenches and unrolling long coils of barbed wire.

Up ahead, the leading trucks had pulled to the side of the road and Olivia noticed that the remainder of the first convoy was there, too. The major in command was standing on the road, talking to another officer. The officer was pointing off to the right, past a huge cluster of large fuel-storage tanks, and the major nodded and began giving orders to the men gathered behind him. Some broke away and came down the line of trucks.

"Okay, lads," one of them shouted as he reached Olivia's truck. "Holiday's over. Orders are to dig in along the coast down there. The 22nd Brigade's already there and General Bennett wants all us Aussies to stick together."

The men clambered out of the truck, grumbling and cursing quietly. Dave jumped over the side. Then he turned back to Olivia and held up his arms to help her.

Georgia chuckled. "Quite the gentleman, aren't we?" Dave flushed scarlet and Olivia felt for him, but she was glad that some of Georgia's old spirit was back.

She allowed Dave to help her down. How much

older you look, she thought. It was all in his eyes and the set of his mouth. Has it happened to me, too? she wondered. Part of her wanted to look in a mirror. Another part was too scared of what she'd see.

Dave held out his hand. "Good luck," he said, managing a faint smile. It didn't reach his eyes. Maybe it never would again. The thought made Olivia feel terribly sad – for him, for her, for the world and what it had become.

"So where to from here?" asked Georgia.

"Singapore's that way." Dave pointed towards the smoke. "Just follow the road. I reckon you'll be able to get a lift."

"All right!" a sergeant shouted. "Let's form up and get cracking!" His eyes fell on Dave. "Come on, Searchfield!"

Dave gave a small wave, then turned and joined the column of soldiers marching past. He didn't look back.

"Come on," said Georgia, tugging lightly on Olivia's sleeve. "With a bit of luck, we might hit Singapore before it gets dark."

Before it gets dark? The smoke had already turned the sky black. The sun's rays seemed to be trapped beneath it, lending everything an eerie, unearthly glow.

CHAPTER *six*

The girls joined the stream of refugees heading towards Singapore.

The island was flat, so walking was relatively easy. There was no jungle, just low scrub and farmland, punctuated here and there by taller trees. They passed a number of bungalows just like the ones their parents owned in Kota Baharu. They looked deserted.

The sun was red and heavy now. There was no way they were going to reach Singapore before darkness fell.

"We'll have to find somewhere to sleep," said Georgia, squinting at the setting sun.

"Maybe we can get into one of those deserted farmhouses," suggested Olivia.

"You're on. We bunk down at the next farmhouse we pass."

But that turned out to be easier said than done. They walked on for another twenty minutes without passing a single house.

"Looks like we might have to kip down in an army camp," said Olivia, without much enthusiasm.

Georgia shot her a resigned look. Neither of them was keen on the prospect of spending another night with a bunch of smelly men.

"Olivia! Georgia!"

They stopped at the cry.

"Hey! Girls!"

There was no mistaking that accent. The girls looked at each other, checking to see if they hadn't imagined it.

An army lorry squealed to a halt beside them. A woman stuck her head out of the passenger window, her dimly lit face framed by raven black hair.

"Ida!" cried Olivia, hardly able to believe her eyes.

Grinning broadly, Ida flung open the door and dropped down onto the road. "You made it!" she cried, sweeping the girls up in a hug.

A huge, silly grin was spreading across Olivia's face, but she didn't care. "You, too! But . . ."

Ida stepped back, her eyes sparkling in the low light. "How? Hop in and I'll tell you all about it."

Olivia and Georgia piled into the cramped cab, giggling like little girls at Christmas time, and Ida shimmied over against the driver to make room. Lucky he's thin, thought Olivia, looking at the reedy soldier.

"Angus, meet a couple of old mates of mine," said Ida and began introducing them grandly, smiling as stupidly as the girls. "Olivia Dempsey and Georgia

Simmons, meet Corporal Angus McBride of the Royal Argyls."

The driver nodded and put the truck into gear.

"So how did you get away?" Olivia was eager to learn of Ida's escape.

Ida told them that a British mobile patrol had stumbled on her a couple of hours after the girls had left. By that time Sam had died, but miraculously the young nurse was still alive. "Tough little lady that one," said Ida, the awe evident in her voice. "Anyway, they gave us a lift in their Bren gun carrier. Somehow the Japanese had got between us and Kuala Krai so we had to take another route south."

"So that's how you missed us," said Georgia.

Ida nodded. "I guess you didn't make the last train, huh?"

Olivia shook her head and related the events of the last few days.

"Well," Ida said after she had finished. "You're here now. That's the main thing. So, whereabouts in Singapore are your mothers?"

"Kitchener Street," replied Olivia. "It's somewhere in the south-west part of the city apparently."

"Kitchener Street?" Angus spoke for the first time. His voice was surprisingly deep for such a wiry man. "Och, that's not far from Alexandra Hospital, where we're headed."

"Well, that's settled then," announced Ida. "We'll drop you off at your mum's house. Won't we, Angus?"

Angus scowled, regretting having spoken.

"*Won't we*, Angus?" repeated Ida, giving the man a poke in the ribs with her elbow.

"I'm nae a taxi service," muttered the Scot.

"Oh, come on, Angus," Ida said. "You've heard what these girls have been through. Be a good chap, why don't you, and I'll see if I can't fix you up with some medicinal whisky when we get to the hospital."

Angus visibly perked up at this prospect. "Aye, well. It's no too far out o' the way."

Night had fallen by the time they reached the city, but there was plenty of light to see by. Buildings were burning and rubble covered the streets. Soldiers and firemen battled blazes, their long hoses sending up great streams of water that seemed to do little to quell the fires.

Here and there, bodies lay sprawled in the street. "Oh, my," croaked Olivia. "Why don't the people hide in the shelters when the bombs come?"

"What shelters?" snorted Angus. "There are no shelters."

"So what happens when the bombers come?

Where do you hide?"

"A ditch. A cellar if you've got one." He looked out at the street. "Not a lot of these folks have."

Olivia heard Georgia take a sharp breath. Without looking at her, she held on to her arm. She was thinking of her mum, just as Olivia was thinking of hers. Did *they* have a cellar to run to?

Angus turned into another street. Unlike the one they'd just left, it seemed to be free of any devastation. They drove past tall buildings with magnificent arched colonnades that reminded Olivia of the pictures she'd seen of ancient Rome, as if the architects who designed Singapore were trying to echo the glory of an earlier empire.

But now she saw that her first impression had been deceptive. Some of the stonework was blackened by smoke. Other buildings had lost their roofs.

"Well, here we are, girls. Kitchener Street." Angus hung a left into a narrow road, barely wide enough for one truck to travel along. The houses loomed over them like malevolent giants. "What number is it then?"

Olivia's mind went blank.

"Twenty-six," said Georgia. She gave her friend a cheeky smile. "Lucky I came along for the ride, isn't it?"

"Eighteen, twenty . . ." counted Angus, peering out the driver's window. "Twenty-two . . ."

Olivia felt her heart pumping. She was about to see her mother!

"Twenty-four, twenty . . ." The words died in his throat.

"What?" Olivia looked out past Angus. "Oh!" she squeaked. "Oh, no."

"Amazing it was," the white-haired lady was saying. "Only one bomb landed in the whole street. The entire building was demolished, yet none of the others got so much as a scratch."

Olivia wasn't listening. She was looking at the ruin that had once been 26 Kitchener Street.

"But what about the people who lived here?" asked Ida impatiently.

The white-haired lady pulled a face. "I don't think I care for your tone," she said haughtily. "I've been through quite a lot, you know. All of this bombing and what have you. And to have one drop on the house right next door! Right next door!"

Ida took a deep breath. "Please, these girls' mothers were in there."

The white-haired lady's eyes widened with

shocked surprise and she began to huff, trying to cover her embarrassment. "Oh, well . . . They were taken away in an ambulance. They were still alive."

Ida reached out and grabbed the woman's arm. "Which hospital?"

"Well I . . ." The white-haired lady was very flustered now. "Well, I would assume it would be Alexandra. That's the closest."

"Right, Angus, let's get cracking!" Ida ran over and grabbed the two girls.

They arrived at Alexandra Hospital later that night to be told by a haggard-looking nurse that their mothers and Mrs Bathurst had been evacuated on a hospital ship several days before.

"Are they going to be okay?" Ida asked the woman.

The tired eyes scanned the records again. Finally, she nodded. "It would appear so. Mrs Dempsey suffered a broken arm and some broken ribs. Mrs Simmons had a broken leg and a suspected concussion." She looked up and gave them a sickly smile. "They were lucky."

Olivia let out her breath in a relieved whoosh.

The nurse went on to explain that, under normal

circumstances, the women would have stayed at Alexandra or been transferred to another hospital in the city. But orders had gone out a couple of weeks before that all European women and children were to be evacuated as soon as possible. The injured were among the first to go.

"You mean the army doesn't think it can hold Singapore?" asked Georgia, her voice barely a whisper.

The nurse shrugged. "I don't know. They just want to be on the safe side, I suppose. Some stories have come out of Hong Kong about what happened to the women there."

"Thank you, nurse," interrupted Ida, her voice curt. "You've been a great help."

The nurse looked at her sharply, then saw the expressions on the girls' faces. "You can report to Sister Hawtrey in Ward Six on the second floor if you like. She may be able to find you somewhere to sleep."

As they turned to leave, she called after them. "Oh, yes, and you may want to put your names down on the evacuee list. So they can get you out on one of the boats."

Ida nodded her thanks. "Any idea when it's your turn?" she asked in a friendly tone.

The nurse shook her head. "I'll be here to the

end, love. My husband's a policeman in the city. Singapore's our home."

"What did she mean about Hong Kong?" queried Georgia as they climbed the wide stairway to the second floor.

Ida shook her head. "Nothing. She was tired. Don't worry about it."

"But . . ."

"I said, don't worry about it!" snapped Ida.

Georgia looked over at her friend and raised her eyebrows.

Despite the desk nurse's doubts, Sister Hawtrey, a tall, broad-shouldered woman who seemed to be in charge of everyone and everything, did indeed find them somewhere to sleep that night. It was only a couple of thin mattresses on the floor of one of the corridors but, after what Olivia and Georgia had slept on in the last couple of weeks, it seemed like luxury.

It was only after they had settled down for the night, with medical staff continually padding by and talking in hushed whispers, that Olivia's initial euphoria about her mother faded. Now it was replaced by the dark, ugly voice that had piped up in her mind when her father had sent her away. She didn't feel happy any more. She felt betrayed.

Abandoned.

Once again, her mother wasn't there for her, she thought, with bitter self-pity. Just like all the other times. Okay, she was wounded, but she must have known that Dad would send me down here when war broke out. He probably rang her to let her know! She could have insisted on staying. But, oh no, it's always Mother first.

"I'm glad they made it out of here," whispered Georgia.

Olivia felt a pang of guilt, as if her friend had been able to read her thoughts. "Yeah," she replied. "Me, too."

"They'll be waiting for us when we get to Aussie. That's something. At least we'll have someone waiting for us."

Olivia stared up at the ceiling fan rotating slowly in the heavy, humid air. "Yeah. They'll be waiting for us."

The Alexandra Hospital ended up being their home for the next four weeks. It was Ida's idea and Sister Hawtrey didn't seem to mind. After all, she reasoned, there was nowhere else for them to go.

"As long as they pull their weight! This isn't a

children's holiday camp."

They changed beds, emptied bedpans, carted off dirty linen and brought back fresh sheets.

When it wasn't raining, they took wounded soldiers in wheelchairs out into the hospital grounds. On these bright sunny days, Olivia would marvel at the magnificent hospital building. It was only three years old, but obviously the British Empire's nineteenth-century glory days had inspired this architect, too. It was three storeys high, constructed from whitewashed stone that dazzled in the sunlight, and surrounded by rolling lawns dotted with trees and shrubs. Even the occasional bomb crater couldn't dispel the Gothic romance of it all.

By some miracle, no bombs fell on the hospital. Around it, however, the sky filled with more and more roiling black smoke. Eventually, the hospital was swathed in shadow, even when it wasn't raining.

The wounded kept coming in, telling tales of retreat and disaster from the mainland. Every day, more and more Europeans were evacuated.

"You only get one hour's notice to pack up and get to the harbour," the girls had overheard one of the doctors saying.

As she grew more absorbed by her work,

Olivia started to feel good about herself. I'm doing something that actually means something, she thought. Sure, the things she had to do were sometimes pretty foul. But all that went out the window when she saw the faces of the soldiers light up as she took them for walks in the grounds or sat beside their beds during the long, hot nights and listened to them talk about home.

Sometimes, she felt a lump rise to her throat as she listened and she was glad they couldn't see her face in the darkness.

Every day now, they heard the mighty booming of the huge guns that guarded Singapore. The shells whooshed overhead like an express train, exploding somewhere far off on the mainland.

Olivia wondered how long Singapore would be able to hold out.

Food wasn't a problem. There was enough for everyone and then some. In fact, neither Olivia nor Georgia had eaten so well in their lives, even when they were back home. Ida told them that enough food had been stockpiled to last for six months.

"As if we'll be here that long," snorted a soldier in a bed nearby.

Ida told him to shush in a good-natured way, but the look on her face let the soldier know she wasn't joking. They didn't hear another peep out of him.

On the evening of January 31st they heard a distant rumble in the north. The next morning, a soldier came into the ward with the news that the causeway to the mainland had been destroyed by English sappers. All the Allied soldiers who weren't dead or captured were now packed onto the island, waiting for the Japanese to cross the narrow Straits of Johore.

"That's our lot then," muttered one of the wounded soldiers despondently. He rolled over and closed his eyes.

The mood in the hospital over the next week was even more sombre than it had been before. Everyone waited for news that the Japanese had landed. But the days passed, and the Japanese stayed on the mainland. People began to feel a sense of hope.

The news they had all been dreading came on the eighth of February. The Japanese had landed in force all along the northern shore of the island and the Australian, Gurkha and English troops were in full retreat.

Two days later, they could hear the rattle of small arms fire. It was faint and far off, but it was there. Word started to get around that the authorities were looking at getting as many European women and children off the island as they could, as quickly as possible.

"Does that mean the nurses will be sent away, too?" Olivia asked Ida one day as she was helping her put fresh sheets on some of the beds.

Ida was silent for a moment. "Only the army nurses," she replied at last, in a strange, flat tone. "They've ordered us to leave. The civilian ones will stay behind and look after the wounded." She started to pull a sheet tight, then stopped again. Her hands went up to cover her eyes and her shoulders started to shake.

Olivia was aghast at the sudden display of emotion, but Ida stopped as quickly as she had started. "Sorry about that," she said with a sniff. Her eyes glistened with tears, but her cheeks were dry. She went back to making the bed.

Olivia's eyes wandered down the crowded ward, looking at the lines of wounded men and the civilian nurses tending them as gunfire crackled in the distance.

At last, late on the afternoon of February 12th,

the order came for the army nurses, Olivia and Georgia to go to Keppel Harbour, where they would be evacuated to Australia. They were given an hour to pack their bags.

Keppel Harbour was like a medieval vision of hell. The nearby oil tanks and warehouses full of rubber were ablaze, casting a flickering light over a writhing carpet of people, their clothes and faces dark with soot from the billowing black smoke.

The noise was deafening. People yelled. Soldiers bellowed orders. Horns blared as trucks tried to get through the mass of humanity. Sounding above it all was the boom of the huge guns.

Elegant Bentleys and Rolls-Royces, their lovingly polished paintwork now coated with a thin layer of soot, pulled up to disgorge their passengers and were then heaved into the sea to make room for more cars and trucks.

The nurses' trucks edged through the crowd until the press of people made it impossible to go any further without running over someone.

"Out you get, my luvs!" the driver called through the window into the back of the truck. "You walk from here."

Olivia clambered down into the seething sea of humanity. The heat was stifling with so many bodies pressed so close together in the soot-laden air.

"Come on, girls!" bellowed Sister Hawtrey, her voice just audible above the racket. She pointed to an elegant-looking ship nearby. "That's our transport. The *Sultan's Star*."

"Coo," said Ida with a whistle. "Travelling in luxury, aren't we?"

From the little that Olivia could see of the boat above the bobbing heads, it was indeed a beautiful-looking ship – sleek and streamlined compared to the no-nonsense sturdiness of the cargo ships and other transports.

The nurses formed a wedge, with Sister Hawtrey at their head, and carved a path to the *Sultan's Star*.

Captain Simms was worried. There were too many people and too few ships. Already, the *Sultan's Star* was nearing capacity. He'd have to weigh anchor soon, regardless.

The soldiers and military police had formed a human barrier and seemed to be holding their own against the civilians, opening ranks to let them through a few at a time, then closing up again.

But Simms had noticed with growing alarm that an increasing number of Australian soldiers were appearing. Deserters. They had to be, for no orders had been issued to evacuate troops. They were boisterous. A lot of them were drunk. The MPs might be able to hold them back for a while, but not for long.

He saw a group of a dozen or so pushing their way through the crowds. A soldier with bright red hair was leading them. The sight sent a chill of unease down Simms's spine. They were heading towards his ship. Where were those blasted nurses? As soon as they were aboard, he could set sail.

"Here come the nurses now, sir," said his first mate, a balloon-bellied Merseysider by the name of Tomkins.

Simms flicked a look back at the soldiers. It was going to be a close-run thing as to who reached the ship first. "Get ready to weigh anchor, Mr Tomkins."

He looked back down at the crowded docks. Come on, he urged silently. Come on.

Sister Hawtrey's voice shouted encouragement as the group heaved their way towards the ship. Their being nurses cut no ice with this desperate crowd.

Olivia was jostled at every step.

At last they reached the MPs. Once past them, things were a lot less crowded. Even breathing seemed to get easier.

A sailor stood guard at the bottom of the gangway. "Come on. Move along. Move along."

Olivia glanced up at the ship as she filed up the gangway. People of all nationalities lined the railings. At least it's not like Kuala Krai, she thought, remembering Dr Sidhu's tale.

Just as she reached the deck, a shot rang out. Everyone ducked instinctively. Another shot. Olivia looked over and saw a soldier dangling from the bowline of a ship alongside the *Sultan's Star*. An army officer on the dock was shooting at him with his pistol.

The dangling soldier dropped into the water.

"Everything's falling apart," muttered a sombre-looking man in a ship captain's uniform. He caught Olivia's eye and managed a smile. "Come along, miss," he said kindly. "No time to waste."

She joined Ida and Georgia at the railing.

"A disgrace." A tubby old man in a white suit appeared beside them, shaking his sweaty, bald head sadly. "Soldiers of the King turning tail and running for their lives."

An Indian man had joined them by now. He, too, shook his head. "But why do the sahibs do such a thing?"

The tubby man glared at him. "Well, of course, they're not sahibs, my good fellow. They're Australians."

Olivia dug her elbow into Georgia's ribs before she could say anything. But now their attention was caught by a noisy struggle at the bottom of the gangway, and soon a dozen Australian soldiers were surging up towards the deck.

Captain Simms had lost his race.

Corporal Rivers was a little drunk and a lot mean. Four days ago he'd been sitting in a sodden foxhole facing the Straits of Johore. Some idiot had decided that the Australian positions should be set up right next to a swamp and he'd been tormented by mosquitoes day and night.

There'd been more than a hundred men strung out along a 180-metre perimeter. Someone in high command had stuffed up and forgotten to send up enough heavy machine-guns. There were only two in the line, and both of them were dug in too far away for Rivers's liking.

Not that he was a coward, mind. After all, he'd been in the desert, doing his bit for King and Country against the Afrika Korps. He'd seen a lot of mates die out there. Good mates who deserved a better fate than dying in grotty little desert towns whose names no one could even pronounce.

Then the Japanese had declared war and Rivers and his regiment had been snatched up, put on a troopship and sent to Malaya. It had all happened so fast they were still wearing their desert gear, which stood out like a sore thumb in the dark green jungle.

They had landed in Singapore three weeks ago and the top brass had sent them up into Malaya. They'd taken up a position on the main highway on the western side of the peninsula, got surrounded and had to fight their way out. Colonel Anderson, who'd been with them since the desert, ordered them to leave the wounded behind, otherwise they'd all end up dead or captured.

Rivers could have sworn he'd seen tears in the old bloke's eyes when he issued that command. He didn't blame him. The order made him sick to the stomach.

So they'd left more than a hundred of their mates lying in the shade of some rubber trees, with a few medics to take care of them.

When the exhausted remnants of the regiment filed on to Singapore island, they were told to dig in along the Straits of Johore.

They had sat and waited for three days, scratching and sweltering. On the second night, a ghost-like figure emerged from the water in front of them. Somehow, through sheer force of will, one of the wounded they'd left behind had made it back. And he brought with him a tale that fuelled Rivers's anger even more – of the helpless wounded being dispatched by Japanese soldiers.

The medics took the man back to the city. Rivers didn't know if he lived or died.

The attack came on the night of the eighth of February. Someone along the line heard a soft splash and shot up a flare. The shoreline in front of them was alive with Japanese, quietly paddling towards them in wooden dinghies.

There were so many Japanese and the Australians were spread too thin. Next thing Rivers knew, the enemy had snuck in behind them.

That's when he decided he'd done enough for King and Country.

He wasn't alone. That night, the Australian line simply disappeared as soldiers climbed out of their trenches and made their way back to Singapore.

Rivers set off with six mates and they joined up with five men from another regiment.

When they reached Singapore, Ted MacNaught, a big, burly shearer from the Northern Territory, had been the first to spot the liquor store. It was deserted. The owner had obviously taken off. And so the twelve Aussies who had had enough of war got good and drunk.

It was two days before Rivers suggested that they head for the harbour. After all, that was the general idea wasn't it? He had pushed and shoved his way through the press of people. All civilians, he noted with contempt. "Our mates are dying up there to defend you lot!" he yelled at no one and everyone.

A shot rang out and people ducked instinctively. Screams. More yells. Another shot.

"Strewth! Look at that!" Ted was pointing to a ship where an Australian soldier was clambering up one of the bowlines in a desperate effort to get aboard.

The ship was casting off its lines. Already it was starting to move away from the dock.

"We'd better get cracking if we want to get a ship!" said Ted.

The soldiers formed a tight knot and barged their way through. And then they were clear, with a gangway before them.

CHAPTER *six*

Up on deck, the captain and several sailors had formed a barrier. The Australians stood in a line facing them. The air sizzled with tension. A couple of the Australians pointed their guns at the sailors, but it didn't seem to faze the captain any, Rivers noted. He could see from the cool look in the man's eyes that he wasn't one to scare easily.

"Get off my ship!" growled Captain Simms.

"Can't do that I'm afraid, mate," replied Rivers, his casual tone belying the tension he felt.

"You're deserters. I want you off my ship."

Rivers felt his face redden. Deserter. He hadn't really thought about that before. Yeah, well, some might say he was a deserter. But he reckoned he was just an ordinary bloke who'd had enough. "We just want to go home," he said levelly.

"Not on my ship you're not," replied Simms.

A renewed outbreak of noise caused them all to look down at the dock. There were more deserters now. The thin line of soldiers and MPs was buckling under the pressure.

"In about one minute you're going to be up to your neck in Aussie deserters," said Rivers. "And, by the looks of them, they won't be as reasonable as us." He quickly scanned the crowded deck. "I reckon you've got a full ship, Captain. It's time we moved on."

He could see Simms balancing up the options. He knew the captain couldn't risk a mob climbing onto his ship. If that happened, they'd all be lost.

"Very well," snapped Simms. "On the condition that you surrender your arms."

"Never," muttered one of the Australians.

Rivers held up his hand for silence. He looked Simms square in the eye and the man held his stare. "Okay," he said at last. "I trust you." He turned to the others. "Give 'em up, lads."

Olivia didn't realise she'd been holding her breath until she let it out with a relieved whoosh. She watched as the red-headed Australian and his companions handed their rifles over to the sailors.

"A disgrace!" the tubby man protested. It seemed to be his favourite word. "His Majesty's ship being overrun by wild colonials!"

"Oh, give it a rest, Grandpa!" sighed Georgia. "They've given up their guns, haven't they?"

The man regarded her coldly. "Another colonial," he huffed and waddled away down the deck.

Olivia and Georgia looked at each other and burst out laughing. They laughed so hard they couldn't stop. After a while, they couldn't even remember what they were laughing about. People looked at the two howling girls and moved away. And still they laughed, until the tears were rolling down their cheeks and their insides hurt.

They were getting out. They had made it. They'd walked the length of Malaya. They had been shot at and bombed and almost drowned. And they'd come out alive. If that wasn't worth laughing about, what was?

They didn't stop laughing until the ship was almost at the harbour entrance. Finally, gasping for breath, they wiped their eyes and looked back at the city. The sight that greeted them sobered them instantly.

Beneath the night sky, Singapore was burning.

The *Sultan's Star* was a beautiful ship. Built as a luxury yacht for the Sultan of Johore, it was donated to the Royal Navy when war broke out in Europe in 1939 – the Sultan's bit for the war effort.

Now, nearly three years later, the *Sultan's Star* was painted a dull battleship grey and had an anti-aircraft gun fixed to her bow, but she still looked every inch a luxury yacht.

The interior boasted elaborately carved balusters and a sweeping, curved staircase that led below decks. A spacious dining saloon featured a fireplace, incongruous in such a hot climate, and there was a library and huge drawing room, both intricately panelled, with ornate ceilings.

But Olivia and Georgia were oblivious to all that as they sat sweltering on the quarterdeck in the blazing midday sun. It was no use going below decks. It was even hotter down there and the stink from overworked latrines and hundreds of sweating, unwashed bodies was unbearable.

It wasn't much better up here. You could barely move without tripping over someone.

Rivers and his companions had gathered around the anti-aircraft gun and were chatting to the gunners. Several sailors stood at various points on the deck, scanning the skies with binoculars.

Olivia looked at the four lifeboats on their davits for the umpteenth time that day. Four. There weren't enough, she thought. Please don't let the Japanese find us.

They had been lucky so far. Tomkins had explained that Captain Simms was making the journey a little bit at a time, sticking as close to land as possible. They'd seen a few bombers fly past in the distance, but the planes hadn't spotted them. They were after bigger game further out to sea.

Simms's strategy seemed to make sense, but it also made for slow going. After two days' sailing, they had reached the Straits of Bangka that ran between Sumatra and Bangka Island.

Simms received a radio report that the island had just fallen to the Japanese and now there was the risk that they would spotted from the land as well as by air. The lookouts were doubled.

As Olivia and Georgia sat sweltering, Tomkins joined Captain Simms on the bridge. The first mate was shocked at how old and tired his captain looked. It was at times like this that he was glad he didn't have to carry the burden of command.

"Been lucky so far, sir," he said, in a weak effort to cheer Simms up.

Captain Simms's tired eyes shifted away from the horizon and rested on Tomkins. "Let's just pray our luck continues to hold," he said grimly. He looked down on the crowded deck. "For all their sakes."

One of the lookouts near the bow started to wave, and his heart sank. "Looks like we didn't pray hard enough," he muttered to himself.

The sailor pushed his way through the crowd and ran up to the bridge. "Japanese bombers, sir!" he gasped, red-faced and sweating. "Six of them, coming in from the north. Heading right for us."

Simms barked an order to the sailor at the wheel. "Evasive action, helmsman!" His voice was suddenly firm and commanding, as if the tired man of a moment before had been an illusion. "Get the anti-aircraft crew to work, Tomkins. And hand out life jackets!"

Olivia had watched the sailor making his way to the bridge. Please don't let it mean what I think it means, she thought. The harsh ringing of the claxons removed all doubt. They were under attack.

Everyone rose to their feet and shuffled about, confused. Sailors appeared and began to distribute life jackets. Others clambered up on to the lifeboats and threw off the canvas covers.

Olivia could see the bombers now. A group of three black specks, with another three just behind. The anti-aircraft gun started to fire, a dull thump-thump-thump sound, and puffs of black smoke appeared around the specks as the shells exploded.

Olivia felt the ship shift beneath her as the helmsman turned hard to port. A couple of minutes later, the ship turned to starboard. Some of the weaker passengers, taken unawares, stumbled as the ship followed its zigzag course.

The first wave of bombers dropped their loads and Olivia flinched as huge geysers of water erupted on both sides of the ship. Some of the women screamed. Children started crying. And above it all was the steady thump-thump-thump of the anti-aircraft gun. They weren't hitting anything, but they were putting the pilots off their aim. Olivia could see the aircraft jerking this way and that between the blasts.

The first wave of bombers had passed over now and, despite herself, Olivia felt a surge of hope rise up within her.

Now the second wave came in. The third plane was slightly behind the others, flying erratically like an injured seabird. Again the bombs plummeted down. And again they failed to hit the swerving boat.

"Three cheers for the captain!" someone cried.

People began cheering. It had a desperate ring to it, but it was cheering nonetheless.

"Still one to come," said Georgia.

The third plane was almost overhead, its engine making strange, spluttering sounds. Anti-aircraft fire surrounded it but, unlike the other planes, it maintained a steady course.

Olivia's throat went dry.

A bomb, squat and sinister, dropped from its belly. With a shrill whistle, it fell towards the *Sultan's Star*.

Everyone on board simply stood and watched, praying that this bomb, too, would plunge harmlessly into the sea beside them. The ship continued to zigzag, but each turn seemed slower than the last. And the bomb grew larger and larger.

"It's going to hit," Georgia gasped.

With a thunking sound, the bomb disappeared down the ship's funnel. For a long moment, there was silence. Someone gave a mad little laugh.

Suddenly, the *Sultan's Star* reared out of the water as a thunderous explosion ripped through its insides. People were thrown to the deck. Others shrieked as they were flung over the railings and into the sea.

Gouts of flame shot out of the lower portholes. Smoke billowed out of doorways and the ship shuddered as another explosion ripped through her. One of the masts snapped in two with an ear-splitting crack, smashing two of the lifeboats as it fell.

"Quick, put these on!" It was Rivers. He was wearing a life jacket and held two more in his hands. He thrust them out to the girls.

Before the girls could say anything he was off, heading towards a group of sailors who were trying to launch one of the remaining lifeboats. Somewhere someone was yelling, "Abandon ship! Abandon ship!"

The deck began to tilt towards starboard.

Olivia began to cough as smoke came billowing up from below.

"We've got to get to a lifeboat!" Georgia cried.

The deck was tilting even more now, making it difficult to stand upright. A sailor appeared out of the pall of smoke. It was Tomkins. "Get to one of the boats on the starboard side!" He had to yell to be heard above the noise.

He pushed them towards the lifeboat that Rivers had made a beeline for. It was already crammed with people and an officer stood alongside, counting off the occupants with his finger. "Lower away!" he yelled to the sailor in charge of the boat. "She can't take any more!"

As Olivia and Georgia watched, their hearts sinking, the boat disappeared over the side.

Tomkins did a quick survey of the deck, sucking his teeth in dismay. "That's the last of 'em. Looks like we'll have to swim for it."

Another explosion rumbled below decks. Whatever order there had been was completely gone now. It was everyone for themselves. People began pushing, shoving and punching in an effort to reach the side of the ship.

Several sailors tried to restore order, but they were quickly swept aside.

CHAPTER *seven*

"Girls! Come on!" Ida lurched into view and grabbed their arms. "Let's go."

She barged her way through the crowd, pulling the girls after her through the suffocating smoke. At the railing, the sea was surprisingly close, barely two metres away, and churned white by the dozens of struggling people. Olivia caught a glimpse of Sister Hawtrey sitting on a life raft, bellowing orders to two nurses who were helping survivors to clamber aboard. And then Ida gave her a shove and she was over the side.

She hit the water and bobbed quickly to the surface. Something splashed next to her and a moment later Georgia's face appeared, her golden hair slicked flat across her forehead.

The yacht looked huge from here in the water. Flames licked at the quarterdeck and smoke was billowing everywhere. People continued to tumble into the sea.

"Let's move!" said Ida.

"But where?" Olivia looked around. All she could see was masses of people thrashing aimlessly about.

"Just get away from the yacht, for a start. We don't want her taking us down with her."

That got Olivia kicking. The three of them splashed frantically away from the stricken ship, pushing past people and bits of wreckage.

After five minutes, they rested and looked back at the *Sultan's Star*, now blazing from bow to stern.

Olivia took another look around, breathing hard. There! Off to the right! She could see land. But so far away!

"Captain Wright!" a voice boomed across the water. "Thank goodness, you've made it!" It was Sister Hawtrey, bearing down on them in her life raft. "Come on, girls. Paddle! Paddle!" There were a number of nurses with her, using bits of wood as oars.

Before Ida could reply, a vicious snarling sound filled the air, followed by a tak-tak-tak! Olivia recognised the sound and was instantly transported back to that terror-stricken day in the school grounds.

A Japanese fighter plane swooped in across the waves, machine-guns blazing. "You swines!" raged Sister Hawtrey.

The plane banked around and came in for another run. The bullets shot up little fountains of water as they passed through the struggling mass of people.

Still Sister Hawtrey ranted and raved, shaking her fist at the aircraft. It roared straight over them and away. Maybe it was over. Oh, please. Let it be over.

But Olivia's hopes were in vain. The fighter was coming around again and this time she and her companions were straight in its path. She heard the staccato of the guns and saw the fountains appear. The line came closer.

Olivia tried to get the jacket off, but her numbed fingers were useless against the knots. She screamed, something hit her on the side of her head and the world went black.

Her forehead was being patted with something soft and cool. She opened her eyes and closed them again quickly against the glare of the sun. When she opened them again, slowly this time, a face began to take shape above her.

"You're okay," said a familiar voice. "It's just a graze."

Olivia's vision cleared and she recognised Ida bending over her.

"Where are we?" Her throat felt rough and dry.

"We're on a beach on Bangka Island," replied Ida.

Olivia pushed herself up onto her elbows and a sharp pain shot through her head. She winced, but the pain quickly eased into a dull throb.

Survivors, sodden and tired, were scattered about

on the white sand. Others were lying further up the beach beneath the shade of overhanging trees. Olivia could hear their moans and saw clothing splashed with red. Most of the nurses were tending to them as best they could. With no medical supplies, all they could do was offer words of comfort and stroke fevered brows.

She saw that Rivers was there, too. There was no mistaking that wild mane of red hair. There were two other soldiers with him. Captain Simms himself stood slightly off to one side, gazing up at the jungle and then out to sea.

There was one face she didn't see.

"Where's Georgia?"

Ida's eyes clouded and she shook her head. "I'm sorry. We lost her when the planes came in."

A glimmer of hope. "Lost her? You mean you didn't see what happened to her?"

"No, I didn't. But we've been here for two hours. All the survivors from the ship are here now."

"No!" Why was Ida giving up on her friend like this? Georgia was a survivor. Why, right now, she was probably just out beyond the surf, swimming towards them. She had to help her!

Olivia raced down to the water's edge, littered with the debris of the *Sultan's Star*. Life belts. Bits of furniture. The wreckage of a lifeboat.

"Georgia!" she cried, standing on her tiptoes. The effort of shouting rasped her throat and she broke into a fit of coughing. When it had subsided, she tried again. "Georgia!"

She wandered up the beach, yelling out her friend's name, but twenty minutes later she was back where she started, exhausted, her throat raw, still shouting at an empty sea.

Finally, she sank down onto her knees. She didn't cry. She didn't have the energy.

An arm alighted on her shoulder. "Go away," she blurted.

"Olivia, I know how much you loved your friend . . ."

Olivia whirled. "No, you don't! You hardly knew her! You hardly know me!" Why was she saying this? Why was she hurting the only friend she had left?

And then she was crying. For Ho Lap. For her mother and father. For Georgia. But, most of all, she was crying for herself.

Ida stood silently by and watched.

After a few minutes, Olivia's sobs began to ease and Ida touched her on the shoulder again. "There are people up there," she said, nodding towards the jungle's edge. "Badly injured people. They need your help." She squeezed Olivia's shoulder. "*I* need your help."

She didn't wait for Olivia's reply, but turned and walked up the beach. As the warm water washed around her knees, Olivia watched the nurses tending the row of burned and broken people. She could almost hear Georgia telling her to stop sitting around feeling sorry for herself, to get a move on and help.

She stood up, wiped the sand off her knees and walked up the beach to the wounded.

"What do you think, Sister?"

Sister Hawtrey looked at the wounded and then back at Captain Simms. "Well, if we don't get these people to hospital soon, a lot of them are going to die, I can tell you that much."

Captain Simms let out a tired sigh. Everyone watched him in silence as if they all sensed that their destiny rested on what he said next.

Finally, he spoke. "I'll go inland. Find some Japanese and bring them back here. We'll surrender."

"You *are* joking!" It was Corporal Rivers. He stormed up to the ship's captain. "Please tell me you're joking!"

Simms stood his ground. "You heard the Sister. We've no choice. Not if we want any of these poor souls to survive."

Rivers snorted. "There is no way we'll survive if we surrender."

"Don't be ridiculous. We'll be treated as prisoners of war under the Geneva Convention."

The other two Australians laughed, but there was no humour in it. "Look, mate," said Rivers, poking Simms in the chest with his finger. "I was with Anderson's mob when we got surrounded. The officers said the only way we could get out was to leave the wounded behind. They said the same thing as you. That the Japanese would treat 'em as prisoners of war under the Geneva Convention." He turned so that everyone could hear him. "One hundred mates we left behind. One managed to get back and tell us what happened to the rest."

Simms's brow furrowed and he looked at the sky, as if the answer to his dilemma lay there.

Sister Hawtrey gave a quiet cough. "All I'm saying is that many of the wounded will die without medical treatment."

Simms nodded. Slowly, his face brightened. "The Japanese will find us anyway, eventually. But it could be too late for the wounded if we wait for it to happen."

No one said anything. Simms knew the decision was his and his alone. "I'll get help," he said with finality. "Yes. For the sake of the wounded."

Rivers shook his head. "Well, if that's your decision, I'm off."

Simms looked crestfallen. "I can't stop you," he said. "But your help here would be appreciated."

Rivers smiled sadly. "Nothing I could do would make any difference now." He stuck out his hand. "Good luck to you, mate. I hope I'm wrong."

Simms hesitated, then took the man's hand. They looked each other in the eye for a moment. Rivers turned to the crowd. "Whoever wants to come with me can."

The two Australian soldiers got to their feet. Tomkins and another sailor joined them.

"Sorry, Captain," muttered Tomkins. "It just seems like . . . the right thing to do."

Simms smiled and patted his first mate on the shoulder. "I understand, Tomkins. Good luck to you all."

Rivers had turned to leave when Simms called him back. "Here," he said, handing the Australian his pistol. "You'll need it more than we will."

Rivers grinned and gave the captain a wink. "Good on you, mate."

CHAPTER *seven*

The little band straggled off towards the jungle.

"You can go, too, you know," whispered Ida to Olivia.

Olivia was silent for a moment. Oh, she wanted to go all right. She remembered Ho Lap's story about Nanking. And the funny looks the nurses exchanged back at the hospital when they talked about Hong Kong. But she couldn't leave. She had realised that back at the water's edge. It would be like running out. She'd done enough of that.

"I'll stay. I can help here."

A faint smile creased the corners of Ida's eyes. She ruffled Olivia's hair.

Simms announced his plans. He hoped that he would come across a Japanese patrol or, even better, a camp, before too long and bring them back with stretchers for the wounded. He paused for a few moments, still plagued with doubt. Then he turned and strode up the beach.

They watched him disappear around the corner of the bay. And then they waited.

The setting sun had slashed the sky red when the Japanese came. A lone figure appeared at the far end of the bay.

Another soldier joined him and then another. The tiny group conferred for a moment, then came towards them.

One of the soldiers turned and shouted something back the way they had come and, moments later, more soldiers appeared around the headland. On and on they came, spilling out onto the beach in a long line that stretched from the jungle to the shoreline. If Olivia had had any thought of escape, it was too late now.

Private Saito wanted glory. So far, it had eluded him. He had enlisted too late to take part in the fall of Hong Kong. And, for some reason, his regiment had been held back from the attack on Malaya.

Instead, they had leapfrogged Singapore and attacked Bangka Island, which, to Saito's great disappointment, surrendered without a shot fired.

So here he was, a twenty-year-old private in a regiment of veterans, and he hadn't even fired his rifle in anger.

He could tell that some of the older men who had seen action in China and Hong Kong looked on him with open disdain. Some were even taking bets as to whether or not he would run the first time he saw action. He was determined to prove them wrong.

And then, as if in answer to his prayers, the gods had sent an English captain to his camp. It was a pity the man wanted to surrender. He'd heard from Sergeant Mifune that the English would rather give themselves up for a life of shame as a captive than fight gloriously to the end.

"And that is why we shall win," Sergeant Mifune had said. "These English have no sense of honour."

The English captain had told them that a number of soldiers, sailors and civilians were at a beach not far from their camp and that they wished to surrender.

Saito was pleased when Major Ichikawa chose him as one of the patrol to go and collect the prisoners. The English captain had asked that they take stretchers with them, as there were many wounded (Sergeant Mifune was giving the troops a running commentary, as he had spent several years studying at an English university before the war). Major Ichikawa dismissed this with a casual wave, saying it was not necessary.

Puzzled, Saito asked one of his comrades why Major Ichikawa wasn't bothering with stretchers. The soldier regarded him for a moment, then turned away. "You'll see," he muttered.

A grim silence fell over Saito's comrades. It was as if they all shared some secret and he was excluded.

And so Private Saito was none the wiser as he trudged across the sandy beach behind Major Ichikawa. What a man, he thought, watching the officer swagger before him. He had heard many great things from the others about how brave their major was. They said he had single-handedly wiped out an English machine-gun nest in the fighting on Hong Kong.

Saito craned his neck to get a better look at the cluster of survivors. There didn't seem to be many soldiers, he noted. Mostly women and wounded.

He looked down at his rifle. Once again, you will remain silent, he thought despondently.

Olivia counted thirty-five soldiers in all. An officer strode in front of them. He was a slight figure, probably not much taller than Olivia. His appearance was almost feminine, with high cheekbones and delicate features bisected by a thin black moustache. He wore a haughty expression and even managed something resembling an arrogant swagger on the soft sand.

Sister Hawtrey craned her neck. "No sign of Captain Simms," she said.

"Something's wrong." Ida's voice had an edge to it. "They're not carrying any stretchers."

The soldiers had reached them by now. The Japanese officer stood with his legs slightly apart, fingers hooked into his belt, regarding the Europeans with no sign of emotion. He raised his arm in a languid gesture and half the soldiers came forward, prodding the group, separating the able-bodied men from the rest of the group.

Some of the men yelled in protest and the Japanese knocked them down.

Olivia's blood pounded in her ears. This was all wrong.

This was all wrong, Private Saito thought.

Sergeant Mifune gave him a push. "What are you doing? Get over there and help separate the men from the rest of them!"

In a daze, Saito drifted over to where the Englishmen were being herded down the beach. One of them was slower than the rest and Sergeant Mifune angrily indicated for Saito to move him along.

Saito gave him a feeble prod and the man looked at him, his eyes full of fear. Saito gulped. He couldn't meet his gaze.

He heard a frustrated growl beside him. Mifune appeared and hit the Englishman hard between the shoulder blades. The man cried out and staggered forward. Saito winced as if he had suffered the blow himself.

"Stay here," spat Mifune and Saito was left behind as the men were taken across the beach towards the bay they had just come from.

"What's happening?"

Ida shook her head. She reached over and took Olivia's hand in hers. Together, they watched as the men were herded out of sight.

"What is the meaning of this?" demanded Sister Hawtrey.

The officer simply looked at her, a faint sneer on his face.

An expectant hush fell over the remaining survivors. A nurse began to sniffle and the surf thrummed on the sand.

There were shots somewhere in the distance. Olivia's heart was pounding now. Sweat streamed down over her brow and into her eyes. She tried to wipe it away, but her hands were shaking too much.

Ida tightened her grip. "You'll be okay."

No I won't, a tiny panicked voice cried out in Olivia's head. I won't be okay! I'm going to die here!

Olivia had never really thought about dying before, even amid all the bombing and shooting. Somehow it had always seemed that the bombs and bullets had been meant for someone else. But now, these cold-eyed men were right here. Close enough to touch.

The shooting from beyond the bay stopped.

The soldiers returned a few minutes later.

Private Saito heard the shots and, with terrible clarity, he knew why Major Ichikawa had not bothered to bring any stretchers. The realisation appalled him.

He turned, silently pleading to the soldiers who had remained behind. Some of them caught his stare and quickly looked away. But others simply returned his look, as if this happened every day.

The officer strolled over to Sister Hawtrey, indicated the nurses with a lazy gesture and said something to her, then issued a command to his men.

Something prodded Olivia in her back. A soldier was pushing her forward. She gave a little cry of fear. Ida tugged at her hand and glared at the soldier. "We're moving! Don't get your undies in a knot!"

Like the men before them, the nurses and remaining able-bodied women were being herded like sheep away from the wounded. Some of the injured began to cry out plaintively.

Sister Hawtrey strode up to the officer. "Our place is with the injured!" she boomed.

The officer signalled to one of his men, who grabbed the Sister and pulled her over to where the soldiers were jostling the women into a long line facing the sea. The sun was almost below the horizon now, colouring the ocean a rich bluish-grey, speckled with silver. Olivia squinted against the glare.

Her breath sounded unnaturally loud in her ears. Her stomach roiled. Her legs felt light. Don't fall. I will not fall. She looked at Ida, who stood straight and proud, her lips pursed. Olivia felt a pang of shame as a tear rolled down her cheek. She's so brave, she thought. And here I am, quivering and blubbering.

Ida squeezed Olivia's hand tighter. "Be brave, kid," she said. "Don't give these sods the satisfaction."

Olivia took a deep breath. It didn't help much.

The women stood in a ragged line, staring silently out at the peaceful sea. Waves beat a slow cadence on the shore.

The officer yelled an order.

This is it. But there were no shots. Instead, she was prodded again. They were being forced to walk out into the gentle surf.

The line of women became even more ragged as the weaker ones were pushed back by the waves. Salt spray splashed against Olivia's face.

"Chins up, girls!" boomed Sister Hawtrey. "I'm proud of you and love you all!"

Private Saito's hands trembled so much that he could hardly hold his rifle. The soldier next to him, a man who had been a painter before the war, cast him a sympathetic glance.

"Calm down," he whispered.

"But it's not right," Saito managed to squeak.

The ex-painter gave a bitter laugh. "You're a private. It's not up to you to question what is right or wrong. You just obey orders."

Saito stared with wide eyes at the line of women wading out into the surf. He heard the rifles click all around him. Hands still trembling, he managed to feed a bullet into the breach of his gun.

"Ready!"

He raised the rifle to his cheek and peered down the sight. Sweat stung his eyes.

"Fire!"

For the first time since the war started, Private Saito fired his rifle.

Olivia stayed firmly focused on the disappearing orb of the sun. The glare hurt her eyes.

"Dive!" urged Ida. "Pretend you're hit and dive! Swim as far out as you can!"

Olivia took a deep breath and plunged beneath the water.

She kicked forward. She didn't have a clue what direction she was going in. Or even if she was underwater at all. What if her back was still showing? She dived deeper until her face smacked against the bottom and the air burst out of her mouth.

She kicked upwards and broke the surface, then gulped and dived again. Don't panic. Just keep swimming out. Maybe the glare on the water will make it hard for them to see me.

A quick snatch of air and then down again. That was the way to do it.

She surfaced again. Her feet could no longer touch the bottom. She trod water and risked a few seconds to get her bearings. She was at least fifty metres offshore by now.

The swell was hiding her from the soldiers on the beach. Good. I don't have to go out any further. I can swim along the coastline now. Then get ashore! And then . . . what?

Everyone I know is dead. I'm completely alone. Maybe I should just give up now.

The thought repelled her and she started to dog-paddle parallel to the shoreline until the bay was out of sight. Her arms grew leaden and even the simple act of treading water became difficult. She knew she would have to make it to shore now or drown.

The sun had set and the moon had risen. The shoreline was a dark shadow against the night sky. She struck out towards it with a tired, clumsy stroke. A few minutes later, the swell began to carry her in and soon she felt the reassuring sand beneath her feet.

She managed a few steps up the beach and then fell to her knees. Can't stay here. The Japanese will find me. But I'm so tired. Maybe just a quick rest and then I'll carry on.

She let herself slump forward. She was asleep before her face hit the sand.

Something cold and hard poked at her stomach. Olivia opened her eyes and her heart jumped to her throat.

It was daylight. Two Japanese soldiers stood over her. They looked so young and awkward in their uniforms. Their rifles seemed almost too big for them to carry.

Olivia heard someone yelling something. She sat up and looked beyond the two soldiers. A long motorboat was anchored a few metres offshore. A soldier was striding up the beach, the bottom half of his uniform soaking wet. He was shouting and waving his arms. He looked older than the other two. Obviously the one in charge. Whatever he was saying made the two younger soldiers look at each other with uncertainty and then glance down at Olivia. The prodding soldier yelled something at her and gestured with his rifle for Olivia to get to her feet.

Olivia knew they weren't here to take prisoners.

CHAPTER*seven*

And, with that realisation, all her fear was swept away. In its place came a strange, empty feeling. Nothing mattered any more. She looked directly into the soldier's face and pushed the gun away.

The soldiers seemed taken aback. They gulped and sweat poured down their faces.

Then the older Japanese was there. He growled and, as he went for his holster, a shot rang out. The shirt near his shoulder puffed as if a sharp breeze had disturbed the fabric. He shrieked and clutched at his wound.

Olivia looked around in confusion. Five men had emerged from the jungle and were running towards them. Rivers! The Australian was in the lead, Simms's pistol in his hand.

The young Japanese soldiers turned to face the threat, but the sudden appearance of an enemy had unnerved them. They threw aside their weapons and ran. The wounded soldier hurled screams at their retreating forms until a bullet kicked up the sand at his feet and suddenly his courage melted away, too. Holding his shoulder, he staggered after his fleeing comrades.

Rivers skidded to a halt next to Olivia. He pointed his pistol at the retreating Japanese and pressed the trigger. The hammer clicked on an empty chamber.

"Ah, sod it!" he growled. He flung the now useless pistol at the enemy. "And don't come back, you sods!" he bellowed after them.

The two other Australians rushed past him, heading for the boat.

"That's our ticket out of here!" one of them yelled happily.

Rivers gave Olivia a quick look, then trotted off after his companions. Olivia knelt in the sand, shaking, as Tomkins walked up to her, huffing after the exertion of running across the beach. He peered down at her intently.

"You okay, miss?"

Olivia nodded dumbly.

Rivers and the other two Australians had waded out to the motorboat and clambered aboard. One made his way to the wheel and looked across at his companions with his eyebrows raised in mute enquiry. The others shrugged back at him.

"Oh, blimey!" muttered Tomkins as he watched the men on the boat. "Typical landlubbers."

Olivia got to her feet as another sailor approached. "You all that made it?" he asked.

Again, Olivia just nodded.

There was an awkward moment as they both stood there in silence.

"Come on," the sailor said at last. "We're out of here."

He followed Tomkins as he waded out to the boat. Olivia watched them go. She wanted to follow. But somehow she just couldn't move.

Tomkins had got the boat started, but Olivia just stood and watched. It was as if they all belonged to a different plane of reality.

Rivers waved at her. "Come on!"

Why bother? They were all going to die anyway. And, even if they did get through, what was waiting for her at the other end?

She just wanted to sit down on the sand and cry.

"Come on, Olivia. We can't wait here all day."

Olivia turned.

Georgia stood there, smiling at her.

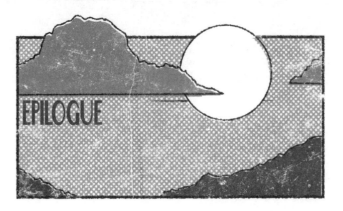

EPILOGUE

Olivia watched the waves roll past the launch in the moonlight. She closed her eyes and let herself be lulled by the gentle, rhythmic motion of the boat.

She was exhausted, but she knew she wouldn't sleep. Not for long, anyway. As soon as she drifted off, the shots would come. And the screams. And she'd wake, soaked in sweat.

So she dozed, and was content with that.

All around her, the world was at war. If only she could stay here forever.

As it had many times over the last two days, her mind drifted back to the events since leaving Bangka Island. Georgia had been washed up two bays along and had hidden in the jungle.

Rivers and his men had found her. After rescuing Olivia and seizing the launch, they'd headed out to sea. They kept a Japanese flag flying at the stern, just in case any low-flying aircraft came by.

The ruse worked. For two days and nights, the small craft puttered along unmolested. As luck would have it, there were two extra drums of fuel on board. Tomkins reckoned there was enough to follow the coast of the Dutch East Indies until they reached Timor, then cut south to Darwin. The food and water should last, too, if they were careful.

It was a hope. And, right now, that was all they could ask for.

Georgia and Olivia were sitting on the bow of the motor launch, their backs against the small cabin.

"Do you think we'll make it home?" whispered Georgia.

Olivia opened her eyes and studied her friend's profile in the soft moonlight. She was surprised to see her cheeks were wet with tears.

She felt tears sting her own eyes and blinked them away.

Home. That was back in Kota Baharu. Wherever they were going now, it wasn't home. She thought about her mother and father. Were they still out there somewhere, waiting for her?

"They're okay. I know they are." Georgia wiped her nose with the back of her hand and looked over at Olivia.

The tears were gone now. She winked. The old Georgia, back again.

Olivia shuffled over and put her arm around her friend's shoulder and they sat in silence, staring at the horizon, stretching vast and empty before them.

"We're going to be okay," whispered Olivia.